Pawprints in the Snow

By Laurie Gifford Adams

Illustrated by Nissa Burch

Table of Contents

Dedicated to all the animals waiting in shelters and foster homes for their forever homes, and to those homeless in the wild. They all just want to be loved and have a place to call home.

With special thanks to:

Jim Adams, Vonnie Alto, Dusty Blumbergs, Dorothy Callahan, Michelle Caward, Laura Chaba, Holly Gustafson, Amanda Harris, Ellee and Charlotte Kluis, Emily Kuryla, Lorraine Lander, Amanda, Abigail, and Ryan Lockwood, Nicole Martinez and family, Mary McConnell, Jane Morris, Melissa Newcomb, Kris Norris, Erin, Michael, Griffin, and Jameson Obi, Cathy Reed, Debbie and Steve Wlodarczyk.

Chapter 1

A MYSTERY

"Ruff! Ruff! Ruff!"

Abby's head snapped up from the snowball she was rolling. Her dog, Mollie, dashed back and forth in front of the big barn doors.

"Mollie! What are you barking at?" Abby asked.

"A-roooo!" Mollie howled with her nose in the air.

Abby's younger brother, Ryan, stopped rolling the ball for his part of the snowman they were building.

"Why is she acting so crazy?" he asked.

"I don't know," Abby said.

Mollie pushed her nose under the small gap in the barn doors.

"Ruff! Ruff!" Mollie barked again. She raced across the snow to the pine trees at the side of the barn. "Ruff! Ruff! Ruff!" The black dog circled the tree under the branches.

"Mollie, what are you after?" Abby asked, jumping up. Her snow pants crinkled as she jogged toward the tree.

She peered through the pine branches, but there was too much snow on them to see.

Mollie's bark turned into whining. Her tail swept the snow into white clouds. Suddenly she backed out fast.

Abby's heart beat faster as she backed away, too. Her imagination took over. What kind of animal could run up a tree? Not a rabbit. A raccoon? A squirrel? Something bigger? What if it was a skunk? Could skunks climb trees? She didn't want either of them to get sprayed!

Mollie whined again and stretched her nose as high as she could. White puffs of frozen air came out with each sniff.

Mollie trotted back to the tree and jumped against the trunk. Little piles of snow from the branches plopped on her black fur. She shook, sending snow everywhere.

Abby threw up her arms to block the snow from hitting her face. At the same time, she was startled by flapping above her head. She ducked just as a big bird swooped out of the tree.

"Silly girl," Abby said. "Were you getting all excited about a bird? Come on." She patted her leg again, but Mollie ignored her.

"Fine! You chase all the birds you want, but you're going to be busy with so many birds from Mom's feeder."

Abby's boots crunched in the snow as she returned to Ryan. He sat with his arms crossed on the first snowball they had rolled.

"It's about time you came back to help," he said. "I don't want to make this snowman all by myself."

"Sorry, but I wanted to know what Mollie was so excited about," Abby said. She patted the big snowball under Ryan.

"This is good for the base of the snowman," she said. "Let's keep going. You roll the head, and I'll finish the middle section."

"Okay." Ryan slid off the snowball. He got on his knees and gathered two scoops of snow between his mittens. "This is going to be the best snowman ever!"

She looked back toward Mollie who was pacing between the barn and the trees. At least she wasn't barking anymore.

Abby turned away, distracted by the way the sun sparkled off the new snow. It looked like diamonds all over the yard. A tingle of excitement fluttered in her stomach. She'd been crossing off the days on her calendar since Thanksgiving, and now it was finally December.

Which meant Christmas was just three and a half weeks away! Finally!

"Are you going to do anything over there?" Ryan called, interrupting her daydreaming.

"Oh, sorry," Abby said. She moved closer to the barn where the snow was fresh and fluffy and dropped to her knees.

She scooped up snow and packed it between her mittens. Her snowball needed to be solid and bigger than Ryan's. Each new layer of snow was packed, then she dropped the ball and added more. With each roll, it grew bigger and bigger. Soon it was big enough to roll along, creating a path in the snow. The path led right to the barn.

It was then that she saw something in the snow. In front of her were small pawprints. They were too little to be Mollie's.

Abby squinted against the reflection of the sun to study the shape. She thought of one of her favorite science lessons in second grade. Her teacher, Miss Loftus, had taught everyone how to identify common animal footprints. The class had learned that if there were no claw marks in the print, then it was a cat's pawprint because cats retract their claws when they walk to keep them pointed and sharp.

No claw marks were visible at the end of the toes. She was positive these pawprints belonged to a cat.

Abby left the snowball and followed the pawprints until they stopped at the barn door. There was a space as big as a basketball at the bottom of the two sliding doors where a part of the wood had rotted. It was just big enough for a small animal to squeeze through. A small cat would definitely fit.

She grabbed the handle on the left door and used all her muscles to slide it open. When the rollers at the top squeaked, she cringed and paused. She peeked around the edge. If a cat was inside, she didn't want to scare it away.

The sun shone through the high windows to light up the inside of the barn, helping Abby see clearly. She looked toward the stacks of hay on one side.

Nothing.

She tiptoed in. The horses — Sasha and Lacey — nickered at her. She stepped up on a bale of hay next to their stalls to peer in.

"Have you seen a kitty in here?" she asked the horses. She giggled at her silliness as she imagined them talking.

"Here, kitty kitty," she called softly as she walked toward the hay. She climbed to the top to see if a cat was squeezed in by the roof.

Nothing.

There was also no sign of a cat in the tack room near the saddles. If there had been one in the barn, she was sure it was gone now.

"Abby?" Ryan called from outside. "Are you going to help finish or not? I'm done with the head."

"Coming," she said. She hurried from the barn and closed the door.

"What were you doing?" he asked.

Abby kneeled and pointed at the snow. "There are pawprints here. I think a cat went into our barn. It probably wanted to get out of the cold."

Ryan scooped up the snowball for the snowman's head and walked over to look. "Big deal! They look like Tanner and Chara's pawprints," he said. "Maybe they got out of the house."

Abby shook her head. "No, they were curled up in their beds when we came out. This is a different cat."

"So what! Come on!" Ryan said. "Let's finish our snowman. My fingers are cold."

"Okay." Abby returned to her snowball. The pawprints stayed on her mind as she rolled the ball along the snow until she was next to the first one.

"Here, I'll help you lift the middle," Ryan said. He set the smallest snowball on the ground, then they lifted the snowman's middle in place.

"We make a great team," she said. She picked up the small snowball and put it on top. "This is perfect for the snowman's head."

Ryan jumped up and down with his hands high in the air. "He's taller than me!"

"He is," Abby agreed. She smiled and brushed her mittens together. "Let's make the face and get some other things to decorate it. We can use a carrot for the nose and two potatoes for eyes."

"We can use a shoestring for the mouth," Ryan suggested.

"Good idea," Abby said. "Let's go."

They hurried into the house. A few minutes later, they were back outside putting the face on the snowman. Next, they added a red scarf and a blue knit cap on his head.

"We need just two more things," Abby said. She ran to the tree in the front yard and broke off two twigs. She jammed one twig into each side of the snowman to make arms, then stepped back.

"We should name him," Ryan suggested.

Abby tapped her mitten against her chin and circled the snowman. "Hmm," she said, thinking. "How about Mr. Winter?"

Ryan nodded. "That's a good name." He patted Mr. Winter's back. "I'll see you later, Mr. Winter. I'm going in to get warm."

"Me, too," Abby said as she re-tied Mr. Winter's scarf. "It's almost time for supper."

Suddenly, she stopped with her hands on the knot and stared toward the barn. Did something just run from the barn to the pine trees? While Ryan trudged to the house, she waited. Maybe her imagination was playing tricks on her. Or maybe the cat had a good hiding place in the barn.

There was one way to find out. She knew exactly what she would do.

Chapter 2

THE PLAN

Abby had a plan. She ran into the house to the cupboard where her mother stored plastic bowls from restaurant leftovers. She took a black one and went to the closet where they kept the cat food for Chara and Tanner.

"Abby, what are you doing?" her mother asked as she came from the living room.

Abby filled the bowl, then turned to her mother. "I saw pawprints in the snow, and then I thought I saw something run out of the barn. I think there might be a kitty living there. I want to give it food in case it's lost and hungry."

"I'm sure it has a home somewhere," Mom said.

Abby carried the bowl to the door. "Well, just in case it doesn't, I'll leave a bowl of food for it."

She trudged across the snow, being careful to not spill the food. In the barn, she turned over a big plastic tub and set the bowl of cat food on top of it. She wanted it high enough so barn mice couldn't get it.

"Okay, kitty," she said, looking around again. "If you come back, you'll be all set."

She walked back to the house with Mollie by her side. Big, fat flakes of snow fell faster and faster. She stuck her tongue out to catch some. As they melted, she decided she would come back to the barn after dinner to see if the cat had returned.

Ryan met her at the door. His cheeks were still rosy from being outside in the cold.

"Was the kitty there?" he asked looking past her.

Abby shook her head. "No, but maybe now it will come since I left food and Mollie is in the house."

She left her coat, hat, mittens, and boots in the laundry room. She needed to set the table for dinner and then feed Tanner and Chara.

"There was no kitty in the barn," she said to her mother as she went through the kitchen. "I hope it's not too cold for it."

"Maybe it found its way home," Mom said. "It probably came from one of our neighbors."

Abby put the plates, silverware, and glasses on the table. After she gave Tanner and Chara their kibble, she went to the dining room to do her homework. She tried to concentrate on her math, but she kept thinking about the pawprints in the snow.

During dinner, she watched out the window toward the barn. The horses came out to roll in the fresh snow, but Abby didn't see any other animal go in or out. She used her fork to scoop up mashed potatoes and broccoli, not even caring that she mixed them. Usually, she kept her food separate on her plate. Tonight, she just wanted to finish quickly. Scoop after scoop went in her mouth.

"Abby," Dad said with a stern look, "you need to slow down. You're eating too fast. What's the hurry?"

Ryan picked up a forkful of mashed potatoes and bounced them in the air toward his mouth. "She thinks she's going to catch a cat in the barn," he said.

Dad raised his eyebrows. "We already have two cats."

"I know," Abby said, "but if it's lost it could be scared and cold and hungry. If it comes back, I'll try to find who owns it. I left it food. I just want to help it."

"That's very kind of you," Mom said. "You are always helping animals."

Laurie Gifford Adams

Abby shrugged. "If Tanner or Chara got lost, I hope someone would help them, too."

"You're definitely our animal lover, Abby," Dad said.

It made Abby happy to know she could help animals. Her mom and dad understood how much she cared about all of them. One time she helped a baby bird that fell out of its nest by putting it back. Another time, a baby bunny was separated from its mother and Abby put it near where she'd seen its bed under a bush.

"I still have to feed the horses," Mom said while she buttered her roll. "We can go out together after dinner."

"Can I take something out for the cat to sleep on?" Abby asked as she imagined the cat in the snow. "It's so cold."

Mom nodded. "You can take one of those old, soft blankets that I keep in the washroom."

Excited, Abby clapped her hands. "Yes! I'll make a little bed for it to sleep on."

"You need to eat right now," Dad said, pointing to her plate.

Abby ate the last bites of her potatoes and broccoli, then stared at her mom's plate. The food was

20

disappearing very slowly. Abby fidgeted and squirmed in her chair. Under the table she tapped her fingers against her legs and glanced toward the barn. What if the kitty was out there right now and they were missing it?

In between bites of food, Ryan shared every detail about his day at school. Abby could only think about the cat. She wished Ryan would talk less and eat more. She wouldn't be allowed to leave the table until everyone was finished eating.

Finally, Mom wiped her mouth with her napkin.

"Okay," she said looking at Abby, "Dad and Ryan will clean up. Get your coat and boots. Let's go to the barn."

Abby sprang from her chair. She put on her winter clothes and raced out the door.

More snow had fallen during dinner. When she got to the barn, she saw new pawprints in the snow. Her heart beat faster. She slid the door a little so she could peek inside. When she didn't see anything, she opened the door wider.

"Kitty? Are you here?" she called. Lacey nickered in response, but no cat made a sound.

Abby went to the bowl of food she had left and was excited by what she saw. More like what she *didn't* see. Only a few little pieces were left in the bottom.

She whirled around to see if the cat was anywhere in the barn. If it was, it was hiding.

"Drats," she said, putting her hands on her hips. "Where are you?"

Her mother's boots crunched in the snow as she approached the barn.

"Well? Is it here?" Mom asked when she got to the door.

Abby shook her head. "No cat, but the food is almost gone."

Mom smiled. "If it's eating the food, I'm sure it will be back unless it finds its way home." She went into the tack room and came out with two small buckets of grain.

"What do I do about water?" Abby asked. "I can't leave a bowl. It would freeze."

"Put a bucket next to the horses' heated water tub so the cat can get on that to reach water," Mom suggested.

"Good idea," Abby said. "And I'll leave food again in the morning and check when I get home from school to see if it's gone."

"That sounds like a good plan," Mom said.

Abby went to the door and looked out at the crisp, white snow. Somewhere out there was the cat that kept leaving its pawprints. She hoped it was someplace warm. If not, she hoped it would come back to their barn where she had everything to make it warm and safe. She couldn't wait to check the next day.

Chapter 3

THE VISITOR

After school, Abby leaped from the last step of the bus. The snow crunched under her boots as she raced up the driveway. Her backpack banged against her back. She ran past the house and straight to the red barn. New snow had fallen during the day.

"Hey, Abby, wait for me!" Ryan called as he came off the bus.

"Can't! I'm going to the barn first," Abby said. "I want to see if the cat ate the food."

"Mom said she was making a special treat," Ryan reminded her.

"I'll be right in!" she called over her shoulder. She ran across the snow. All day at school she had watched the clock, waiting for the end of the day. It seemed like the clock had moved extra slow all afternoon.

Now she didn't want to waste another second before she checked to see if the cat had come back.

A few steps from the barn, Abby slowed down. A big smile lifted her cheeks when she looked at the snow in front of the doors.

There they were! Fresh pawprints. Excitement shot through her. The cat had come back. She opened the door slowly so she wouldn't scare it if it was inside.

There was nothing there. She listened but only heard Sasha and Lacey munching their hay.

Abby went to the upside-down tub where she'd left the bowl of cat food. It was empty again, but there was no sign of a cat.

"Where are you kitty?" she asked in a soft voice. She checked the same places she had looked before. There was still nothing. She got another scoop of the cat food she'd left in the tack room the night before and put it in the bowl. She would come out again when her mother came to feed the horses.

She followed the snowy path back to the house. The warm air inside felt good on her cold cheeks. She tossed her backpack onto the bench in the laundry room and flung her coat onto the wall hook.

"The cat ate the food!" she said as she entered the kitchen.

Her mom stood by the counter. "They always come back when there's food," her mom said. Abby spied the hot chocolate chip cookies cooling on a rack. The sweet smell filled the room.

"Mmm, those smell yummy," she said.

"I put a glass of milk and two cookies on the table for you," Mom said. "Wash your hands first."

Mollie trotted into the kitchen. Her tongue hung out of her mouth and her ears were up like she was smiling.

"Hi, Mollie," Abby said as she washed her hands, then headed for the table. "You better not scare the kitty away," she scolded. She slid onto a chair next to Ryan. He had already eaten one of his cookies.

"Maybe the cat is invisible," Ryan said as he pushed his little blue toy car along the table. "That's why you only see its pawprints."

Abby rolled her eyes at his silliness. "It will come back. You'll see."

Abby finished her cookies, then went to her room to read her book for school. She didn't even know how much time had passed when she heard her mother call her.

"Abby! I'm going out to feed Sasha and Lacey, before dinner tonight. Do you still want to go out with me?"

Abby tossed her book on her bed and raced down the stairs. "I hope the kitty is out there," she said. She yanked her purple knit hat over her ears, then zipped her jacket as she sprinted to the horse barn.

She pushed one big door back so she could fit through. Since it was dark in the barn, she flipped the light switch on. The light overhead beamed bright and lit up the barn. Abby froze and stared.

It worked!

A tiger cat lay stretched across the blanket. It lifted one eyelid and peeked at Abby.

Abby didn't dare breathe. She didn't want to scare the cat away.

"Mom!" she whispered. "Come slowly. There *is* a cat, and it's sleeping on the blanket I left."

Abby took a step into the barn. The cat's head popped up.

"Hi, kitty," she said softly.

The cat stood and stretched, opening its mouth in a big yawn. It arched its back and straightened its tail but didn't seem scared.

Suddenly, Mollie raced into the barn and went straight toward the cat.

"Oh, no!" Abby said, trying to step between Mollie and the cat.

But she was surprised when the cat didn't run. Instead, she stretched her nose to sniff Mollie's nose then rubbed against Mollie's front leg.

"Look, Mom!" Abby said. "The cat and Mollie are friendly."

Mom nodded. "I have a feeling these two have met before. They do seem to like each other."

The cat purred and rubbed against Mollie's chest like it was proving Mom was right.

"Aww, you're so pretty." Abby started toward the cat, but her mom gently grabbed her arm to stop her.

"We need to be careful when we approach it," Mom said. "We don't know this cat."

Before Abby took another step, the cat jumped off the bale of hay. It trotted to Abby and rubbed against her boot.

"Meow!" The cat looked up at Abby. "Meow!" it said again.

"He's so pretty," she said.

Her mother reached out her gloved hand and the cat rubbed against it. "I think *he* is a *she*," Mom said.

Abby kneeled to pet the cat with her glove. "Hello, pretty girl," she said. "Do you like the bed I made for you?"

The cat purred and rubbed against Abby's legs again.

Abby looked up at her mom. "Can we keep her? I think she likes me."

Her mom tipped her head the way she always did when she was going to say no.

"She might be lost. There might be someone who loves this kitty and misses it. We should see if we can find her owners first."

"But, if she doesn't have a home, can we keep her?"

Mom smiled. "Why don't we make some calls, hang up posters, and post it on the internet. If no one claims her, then we can talk about what happens next."

Abby patted the top of the cat's head. She wondered if it was mean to hope the kitty didn't have a home.

Chapter 4

KITTY GETS A NAME

That night Abby and Ryan made posters and she heard her mother calling neighbors. No one was missing a cat.

Over the next few days, as soon as she got home from school, Abby asked her mother if anyone had called about the cat. No one did. Each day she got more excited that maybe this cat would become hers.

Saturday morning when she took the food out to the cat, Abby made a decision. She sat on the bale of hay and the cat climbed onto her lap. Abby stroked her head and back. The cat purred and rubbed against Abby's coat sleeve.

"I can't keep calling you cat or kitty. You need a name," Abby said, giving the cat a hug. She thought about Christmas. It made sense to give the cat a name for the season.

"What about Merry?" she said, "Or, Snowflake." She petted the cat. "No, you're not white, and Merry doesn't fit you."

She set the cat on the blanket and stepped away so she could look at her from a distance. This kitty needed a special name. And, then it came to her.

"Noelle! That's it! You look like a Noelle."

The cat looked up and meowed.

"You like that name?" Abby asked. She went back and picked up the cat, hugging her against her coat. "I'm telling everyone that you have a name now. Welcome home, Noelle."

Noelle purred and pressed her furry face against Abby's chin.

The decision was made.

For the next few days, Noelle stayed in the barn. Then things changed. Every time Abby left her, Noelle scurried out of the barn ahead of Abby and scooted into the open garage.

Abby picked up Noelle and carried her back to the barn. Then, she closed the big barn door as fast as she could and ran toward the house. But the cat squeezed through the small, rotted area under the door and ran faster than Abby. Every time, Noelle beat her to the garage. Some days they went back and forth five or six times.

Today before Abby could grab her again, Noelle climbed on a shelf in the garage where a green tent was folded and curled up on it.

Abby put her hands on her hips and tried to look stern.

"Noelle, it's warmer in the barn with the horses. Why do you want to be in the garage?"

Noelle licked her front paws, stretched, and curled into a ball. Her tail wrapped around her body until the tip touched her nose.

The door to the house opened and Dad looked out at Abby.

"Hey, Abby. What are you doing?" he asked.

"Noelle keeps following me from the barn and wants to sleep in the garage," Abby explained, "but I'm afraid it's too cold."

"Well, then we'll leave the garage door open a little at the bottom so she can come and go," Dad said. "That way if she wants to go back to the barn where it's warmer, she can."

He pressed the button to open the door just enough for Noelle to be able to scoot underneath.

"Meow!" Noelle said before closing her eyes to go to sleep.

Abby giggled. "Does that mean you like this plan, Noelle?"

"I think she does," Dad said. "She looks comfortable. Why don't you come in?"

Abby started to follow him in but stopped and looked back at Noelle. Even with her coat on, Abby shivered.

"I'll be right in," Abby said.

She went back to the barn, took the blanket from the bale of hay, and carried it to the garage. She set up Dad's small step ladder next to the shelf and climbed up to Noelle.

"Here, Noelle," she said, moving the cat off the tent. "This will be warmer for you." Abby fluffed the blanket on top of the tent, then set Noelle back on it.

Noelle circled on it three times before she laid back down. She purred and stretched one paw to touch Abby's hand.

"Are you thanking me?" Abby asked. She petted Noelle's paw. "You're welcome. Good night, kitty"

Abby climbed down the step ladder and put it away. Just before she turned the light off and went inside, she turned back to look at Noelle.

"I love you kitty."

And, in her heart, Abby knew that she would do whatever she could to make sure Noelle was warm and safe for as long as she was with them.

Chapter 5

A SURPRISE FOR NOELLE

The next day at school, all Abby could think about was Noelle in the cold. Instead of going to recess she got permission to go to the library. She knew exactly what she was looking for: a book on how to care for cats. Since no one had claimed Noelle, Abby hoped her mom and dad would let her keep the homeless cat.

That night after dinner, Abby went to her room to get the cat book. She joined the rest of the family in the living room. Dad sat in the recliner reading the newspaper, Mom was pulling yarn from her knitting bag, and Ryan was putting together his wooden train track.

Tanner laid across one end of the track.

"You can't stay there," Ryan said to him as he added another piece in front of the cat. He set a small train on the floor next to him. Chara pounced on it, then swatted it, sending it flying across the carpet.

"Mom!" he cried. "These cats are in my way."

Mom's needles still clicked together as she glanced up. "If you find something else for them to play with, maybe they'll leave your train alone," she suggested.

"Here, I'll get them away," Abby said, grabbing a long wand with a feather on the end from the cats' toy box. She wiggled the end of it in front of the cats, then slid it across the floor. Both cats chased it, then rolled and played with it behind a chair.

"Thanks," Ryan said, already distracted again by his track building.

Abby laid on her stomach on the floor and opened the cat care book to chapter three since she had started reading it in school. She was on chapter four when her father interrupted her reading.

"Abby, I see the cat has made herself at home in the garage," he said.

Abby set her book on the floor and sat up to look at him. "No one has claimed her, so I named her Noelle. I'm reading this book to learn how I should take care of her."

Dad laid the newspaper on his lap. "That's good. I've noticed that you've taken very seriously the responsibility to take care of Noelle."

"Oh, I have," Abby said. "I'm so worried about her. It's freezing in the garage. I gave her a fluffy blanket, but when I'm warm inside, it makes me sad that she's out there in the cold. Can I bring her inside?"

Dad shook his head while folding the paper.

"No, we already have two cats and a dog inside, but I have an idea. Put on your coat. We're going shopping."

Abby scrambled to her feet. "Right now? Shopping for what?" she asked. Her father never went shopping after dinner.

Dad smiled a big smile and winked at her. "It's a surprise. You'll see."

Little bubbles of excitement danced in Abby's stomach. She couldn't even imagine what this surprise could be. She snatched her coat from the hook in the hall and put it on as she went through the door to the garage. She glanced toward the shelf, and there lay Noelle in a ball, trying to keep warm.

"See how cold she looks, Dad?" Abby said as a little draft of cold sneaked inside her unzipped jacket.

Dad winked again as he opened the door to his silver truck so she could get in.

"I have an idea to fix that," he said.

Abby climbed into the seat, excitement making it hard for her to sit still in the seat. She buckled her safety belt, trying to imagine what Dad had planned.

Usually, she had lots of questions and things to talk about on rides, but she didn't even know what to say this time. She watched out the window as they drove into town and past their church and stores, all decorated for Christmas. Snowflakes danced around the windshield. When Dad turned into the parking lot for Four Paws Pet Supply, Abby could hardly wait to get out of the truck. The big red sign lit up the snow around the store.

"What are we doing here?" she asked.

"If Noelle is going to live in the garage, we want her to be warm and safe."

Once Dad parked, Abby scrambled from the truck. They walked to the aisle that had shelves of cat food, litter, and toys. Then they turned down another aisle.

"Look at this," Dad said, pointing to what looked like big dollhouses. "These are heated houses for cats. Do you think Noelle would like one?"

Abby's eyes widened in surprise. "Really?" Something in her stomach fluttered. She grabbed her father's hand.

"Does this mean I can keep her?" she asked, looking up at him.

Dad shrugged. "It doesn't appear that anyone is going to claim her, and you've been taking very good care of her. Mom and I think Noelle is an early Christmas present for you."

Abby let go of his hand and jumped up and down. "Yes! Yes! Yes! I can't believe it!" She threw her hands around his waist. "Thank you so much! And I know Noelle would thank you, too."

Her cheeks hurt from smiling so much, but she couldn't stop. "This is the best day ever."

"I know you're excited," her dad said, "but the store is closing soon. You need to pick out a house for Noelle."

Abby studied the little houses on the shelves. There were so many different sizes and colors that it was hard to choose. As she looked at each one, she tried to picture Noelle in it. Finally, the one on the top shelf with a pattern of leaves on the outside caught her attention.

"Can you take that one down from the shelf?" she asked, pointing.

Her father took it down and held it for her to look at. She bent to look inside and moved her hand across the fluffy, soft floor.

"This is the one," Abby said, smiling. "It's perfect for her! Noelle will love it and she'll be so cozy and warm."

"You're sure?" her father asked.

She nodded. "I'm very sure."

"Let's get her a heated water bowl, too," Dad suggested.

"That's a great idea," Abby said. "It's important for her to have water with her food. It's so cold that a regular bowl of water would freeze."

"They're right over there," the cashier said, pointing down the next aisle. "That's one lucky cat."

Dad laughed. "She certainly knew what house to pick."

Once outside the store, Abby skipped to the truck while her father carried the little house. She knew Noelle would love it.

A little while later when they drove in the garage, Abby looked toward the shelves, Noelle was curled up on the tent on the shelf, right where she was when they'd left.

"Noelle," she called as she climbed from the truck, "wait until you see what we have for you. You're going to love it."

Abby coaxed the cat down from the shelf, then picked her up to cuddle her against her jacket. She waited while her father made room for the house on a lower shelf. Behind them, the door to the house opened. She looked over her shoulder and saw her mom and Ryan in the doorway.

"What did you get?" Ryan asked.

"Noelle has a nice warm house," Abby said, nodding toward the shelf. "Mom and Dad said I can keep her."

"You get your own cat?" Ryan said. "You're so lucky!"

"Noelle is the lucky one," Abby told him. Then, she turned back and whispered, "You have your forever home, kitty,"

Noelle flicked her ear back and forth, then looked up into Abby's eyes. "Welcome home," Abby said.

Dad plugged in the cord for the heater in the cat house, then he stepped back.

"Okay, it's ready for her," he said. He rubbed his bare hands together, and his breath made a cloud in the air. "Go ahead and let her try it out before we all freeze out here."

Abby stepped closer, and Noelle squirmed out of her arms. Was the cat excited about her new house? Abby held her breath while Noelle sniffed every inch of it. She hoped her new kitty would feel safe and comfortable in it.

She pressed her hands together when Noelle poked her head through the opening, hoping she would go in. Instead of going into the soft, warm area, the cat backed out fast, almost falling off the shelf.

"It's okay, Noelle," Abby coaxed. "It's yours. You can sleep in there and be warm."

She picked up Noelle, again, and placed her at the little house's opening. Noelle sniffed the floor, then spun around and leaped to the shelf with the tent. She quickly circled then curled up and buried her nose in the end of her tail.

Disappointment tugged at the corners of Abby's lips. Noelle didn't like her new house. Did that mean she wouldn't want to stay?

"Dad, why doesn't she like it?" she asked, fighting tears.

Dad put his arm across Abby's shoulder and pulled her against his side. "Give her time," he said. "I remember when you were little and we bought you your first real bed. For two nights we put you to bed, and when we left the room, you dragged your pillow and blanket onto the floor and slept there. When we asked you why, you said it was because it was different. You just needed to get used to it. I bet Noelle will be the same way."

Abby couldn't help feeling worried. "But I don't want her to freeze."

"She knows the house is there, and she can go to the barn," he said. "Just like you, she has to get used to something different. Give her time."

Abby turned to her mother in the doorway.

"Do you think it would be okay if I put something of mine in the house?" she asked. "Maybe then she would feel less lonely out here."

"I think that's a super idea," her mom said.

Abby ran into the house and dug out her old, fluffy purple scarf from the closet. She ran back to the garage and laid it along the inside wall of Noelle's new house.

"Noelle likes me. Maybe if something smells like me, she'll feel safer and snuggle with it," Abby said.

Dad squeezed her shoulder. "I'm proud of your thoughtfulness."

"I just want to take good care of Noelle, Dad."

"You're off to a good start, Abby. Now it's up to Noelle if she wants to take advantage of your kindness. Let's go to bed. You can check on her in the morning."

Even though she didn't want to leave Noelle, Abby went inside. She checked one more time after brushing her teeth, but Noelle was still on the tent.

Abby's shoulders sagged as she trudged up the stairs to bed. It was going to be a long night.

As soon as Abby woke in the morning, she raced down the stairs and opened the door to the garage. She looked at the folded tent on the shelf, but it was empty. Then, she looked at the little house, and her heart swelled.

Noelle sat inside, and she looked warm and happy. "Aww, Noelle, you like your house!" Abby exclaimed. Noelle meowed like she agreed.

Abby took her more food and water, then closed the door and went back to her room to get ready for school.

Noelle is really mine, she thought. She couldn't wait to tell her teacher and friends about her early Christmas present.

Chapter 6

MISSING

Every morning before she had her own breakfast, Abby went to the garage to take care of Noelle. She refilled her food and water bowls.

As she passed her mother in the kitchen, Abby said, "Noelle must have been starving when she came here. She eats a lot of food."

Mom took a carton of orange juice from the counter and put it in the refrigerator. "She was thin when she came here," Mom said. "It's good to see her getting plumper."

Several days after Noelle moved into the garage, Abby woke up a few minutes late on a school day.

"Oh, no!" she said, tossing back her blanket. She jumped out of bed and threw on a sweatshirt and sweatpants.

When she ran from her room, she almost collided with Ryan at the top of the stairs.

"Hey!" he said. "Be careful! You could have knocked me down."

"Sorry!" she said, rushing past and down the stairs. "I'm late, and I still have to feed Noelle."

"Good morning, sleepy head," Mom said as Abby ran through the kitchen toward the garage. "Do you want a pancake for breakfast?"

"Sure," Abby said, pulling open the garage door. "I'll be back in just a few minutes. Need to take care of Noelle."

The winter air cut right through her sweatshirt. Goosebumps jumped out all over her body. She was glad Noelle's house was heated.

From the doorway she couldn't see Noelle in her house. Since it was so cold, Abby thought Noelle was probably curled up away from the small doorway.

"Hey, kitty, sorry I'm late," she said as she approached the shelf with the house.

Usually, Noelle poked her head out and meowed when Abby arrived. Today she didn't.

"Noelle," Abby said as she peeked inside.

The cold air in the garage made her breath come out in clouds. Those clouds went right into the little house.

The empty house.

Abby stepped back and looked around. "Noelle? Are you here?"

When Abby noticed Noelle's bowl, her throat tightened. It was still nearly full of food from last night.

"Noelle? Kitty? Where are you?" Abby called, looking all over the garage. There was no sign of Noelle.

Abby opened the garage door and looked outside. It had snowed overnight. She saw her mom's footprints from when she did chores, but there were no new pawprints in the snow. That meant Noelle hadn't slept in her house all night and hadn't gone to the barn this morning, either.

Abby turned and hurried into the house.

"Mom?" she said as soon as she opened the door, "did you see Noelle this morning?"

"No," Mom answered. "She wasn't in the garage when I went to the barn."

"She didn't eat her food last night," Abby said. "She always eats all of her food at night."

A chill ran up Abby's spine. What if Noelle was hurt somewhere? What if she was lost? Without any tracks to follow, she didn't even know where to look. What if Noelle didn't like her anymore?

"You're sure she wasn't sleeping in the barn?" Abby asked.

"I'm sure," Mom said as she set down the plate with a pancake for Abby. "Maybe she's just out hunting."

"I hope so," Abby said. She wanted to think that's what happened, but she couldn't help but worry. Usually she loved pancakes, but today she could only eat a few bites before she carried her plate to the sink. Her imagination was already thinking of all the things that might have happened.

And none of them were good.

That afternoon, as soon as the doors to the school bus opened, Abby flew down the steps. All she'd thought about all day was getting home to see if Noelle had come back.

She raced into the garage and went straight to Noelle's little house.

It was empty, and her food bowl was still full.

"Where are you?" she mumbled as she turned to go into the house. She found her mom in the office finishing a task for work.

"Did you see Noelle today?" Abby asked before even taking off her coat. She let her backpack slide to the ground.

"No, I'm sorry, Abby. I've been checking, but she hasn't been back all day."

Abby's eyes filled with tears, and she felt hot, but she didn't think it was because she was wearing her coat in the house. A big lump filled her throat, and her bottom lip quivered.

What if Noelle was gone for good?

"Why don't you have a snack, then do your homework," Mom suggested. "I sliced up apples. We'll go outside after that and call for her. Maybe she'll hear you and come back."

Abby felt a hot tear slip down her cheek.

"But, what if she doesn't?" she asked. "What if I never see her again?"

Mom stood and pulled Abby into a hug. "We're going to think positively," she said. "Outdoor cats do this kind of thing all the time. When she gets hungry, she'll be back."

Abby stepped away and unzipped her coat. "I hope you're right." Apples were one of her favorite snacks, but right now, nothing would taste good.

She hung her coat in the laundry room, then peeked out into the garage one more time.

"Noelle?" she called. "Noelle, where are you?"

There wasn't a movement in the garage or a kitty's meow. Noelle was missing, and Abby didn't even know where to look for her. She turned and went up to her room to do her homework. It would be hard to concentrate.

Every fifteen minutes after that, Abby checked the garage. It took her longer than usual to finish her homework, but all she could picture was Noelle lost in the cold, or maybe even hurt. A heavy feeling settled in Abby's stomach.

At dinner she picked at her carrots and moved her potatoes and meat around on her plate. Her stomach growled, but she couldn't eat. Ryan chattered about the kickball game his class played in gym. She wished that was all she had to think about.

"It looks like the weather forecasters may be right," Dad said. "They said the snow would begin after sunset."

Abby snapped her head toward the window. Snowflakes were already building up on the thin ledge.

"Are we getting a lot of snow?" she asked, worried about Noelle.

"We might get almost a foot," Mom said.

"Snow day?" Ryan asked excitedly.

Mom nodded. "Probably. You'll have to make another snowman since the one you built last week melted."

"It's going to be pretty windy," Dad said. "They said a lot of blowing snow."

Abby's stomach did a little flip flop. What if Noelle got caught in the storm?

"Mom," she said, setting her fork down. "May I go out one more time to look for Noelle when you feed the horses? She could get lost and freeze in a storm like this."

Dad rested his arms on the table and looked at Abby. "We'll all go outside and look for her. Maybe she'd hear all of us if we called her. But let's not jump to conclusions. She might be safe and warm someplace right now."

Abby slumped in her chair. "I hope you're right, Dad, but I miss her, and I'm scared."

"Let's go now, then," he said, sliding his chair back from the table. "We can clean up later. This is important."

Abby pushed her plate away and rushed from the table. In less than two minutes she had put on all her snow clothes and boots.

She went out into the garage to wait for the others. She hoped she would open the door and find Noelle curled up in her little heated house.

But she wasn't. The wind swept under the small opening of the garage door. Outside, it whistled through the trees. It would only get worse during the night. They had to find Noelle.

Chapter 7

THE SEARCH

The snow was already up to Abby's knees as she struggled through a drift. She, her dad, and Mollie walked one way around the house calling for Noelle, and her mom and Ryan went the other way. They each had a bright flashlight to look under the porch and in bushes.

"Noelle!" Abby called into the wind. The snowflakes hit her face and melted, but the ones on her eyelashes made it hard to see. She swung her light back and forth, hoping to see eyes reflecting in the beam.

"Noelle!" She and her father both called out.

When they met her mom and Ryan on the other side of the house, no one had seen Noelle.

"Let's check the pine trees," Mom said. "We know she likes hiding in the branches."

They spread out and each looked in different trees. Abby pointed her flashlight toward the ground to see if there were pawprints. There were none. Tingles of worry moved along her skin.

"Nothing," Dad said.

"Me, either," Ryan said, now using his flashlight like a light saber. Snowflakes swirled in and out of the beam. Any other time, Abby would have loved to pretend her flashlight was a lightsaber, too, but not tonight. This was no time for fun.

"Let's go into the barn and get warm while I feed the horses," Mom said, "then we can look some more."

Dad slid the big door open, and they filed in. When Mom flicked on the overhead light, Abby looked toward the upside-down tub where she'd left food and water for Noelle. It was untouched. Every hope she had drained out of her.

Ryan used his flashlight to shine light on everything in the barn. The horses. The old bird nests high up on the beams. The spider webs in the corners. He climbed high up on the bales of hay, pretending he was a ninja.

Mom opened the door to the tack room to get the grain. Dad grabbed a bale of hay from the stack and set it on the floor. He cut the blue strings on it and carried hay into the horse's stalls.

Feeling lost, Abby coaxed Mollie next to her on a bale of hay and watched everyone else. She made a list in her head of the places they could still look for Noelle.

She was thinking about checking the deck on the back of the house when suddenly Ryan yelled.

"Hey! I hear a cat."

Abby leaped to her feet. Dad hurried out of the stall, and Mom rushed from the tack room.

"Where?" Abby asked, scurrying up the stack of hay as fast as she could.

"Back here," Ryan said, pointing toward the wall.

Abby slid on her stomach along the narrow space between the hay and the barn roof until she was next to Ryan.

"Noelle?" she called. "Kitty, are you there?"

"Meow!"

It wasn't loud, but Abby knew it was Noelle. Her heart jumped with happiness. Noelle was alive.

"Mom! Dad!" she yelled. "I hear her. She's trapped behind the hay. We need to get her out!" Abby's voice squeaked on the last words.

"Come back down," Dad ordered, holding his hand out to help them. "We're going to have to be careful about how we move the bales."

Abby and Ryan scrambled down from the hay. Dad and Mom both started moving bales, stacking them next to the stalls.

"Noelle!" Abby called again. "Hang on. We'll get you out."

A faint meow from behind the hay was her answer.

Abby squeezed her gloved hands together, wishing there was something she could do to help.

"I hope she's not hurt." She paced as her parents continued to move hay. This felt like a giant game of Jenga. If they pulled out the wrong bale, the hay mow could collapse. And Noelle was somewhere under it.

One by one Mom and Dad carefully chose which bales to move.

"Please be careful," Abby pleaded.

"We're being as careful as we can be," Dad said. He was breathing hard from working so fast.

From behind the bales, Noelle meowed again.

"We're almost to you, kitty," Mom said. "Hold on!"

More bales were pulled out. Abby moved closer, ready to run in if she saw Noelle.

Dad crawled across the lower stack and peered between the hay and the wall.

"I see her," he said. "She's wedged in. Just a few more bales and we'll reach her."

"How did she get stuck back there?" Ryan asked.

Dad backed out, then picked up another bale as he answered.

"She might have been hunting for mice and gotten herself into a tight spot and couldn't turn around, or it's also possible some hay shifted, trapping her."

Abby stared at the last few bales that needed to be moved. "She must be so scared," she said. "Hurry!"

Mom and Dad pulled out five more bales and tossed them to the side. Noelle meowed more. Then, Mom pulled back a bale and Noelle's head poked up above the next one.

"Noelle!" Abby cried.

"Stay back," Dad said. "Let me lift her out in case she's hurt."

He reached in with his gloved hands at the same time Mom pulled away one more bale. Before he could get his hands around her, Noelle sprang from the tight space and ran past him.

"Noelle!" Abby cried, holding her hands out. The cat trotted to Abby and rubbed against her legs. "Are you okay, kitty?" She leaned down to stroke Noelle's back.

The knot in Abby's stomach loosened. She felt like she could take a deep breath again.

"Are you cold? Hungry?" she asked.

As if to answer, Noelle jumped on the tub where the food and water were. She lapped at the water for a long time, then ate all the kibble in the bowl.

"I think the hay insulated her from the cold," Dad said, "but you can see she's hungry and thirsty."

"I'll get her more food," Abby said. She grabbed the bag from the tack room and added more to Noelle's bowl.

Mom kneeled and rubbed her hands along Noelle's body. "She looks like she's okay, but once this storm passes, we'll get an appointment with the vet. If she's going to be your cat, she needs a physical and her shots. There's more to owning a pet than feeding and playing with it."

Abby nodded and sat down on the tub next to Noelle as the cat ate. She couldn't stop the smile that had started as soon as Noelle jumped free.

Chapter 8

UNEXPECTED

"Meow! Meow!"

Abby put her hand on top of the cat carrier that was buckled in next to her on the back seat of Mom's car.

"I know you don't like being in this little cage, Noelle," Abby said, "but if you're going to be my cat and come into the house, we have to know you're healthy."

"Meow!" Noelle cried again.

"We're almost to the veterinarian's office," Mom said from the front seat.

"Meow!" This time it was quieter.

Abby leaned over and looked in at the kitty. "When you get to move in from the garage, you'll be glad we did this."

For the next few minutes Abby talked to Noelle until they reached the veterinarian's office.

"Can I go in, too?" Abby asked when her mom stopped the car.

"Of course," Mom said. She got out of the car. When she opened the back door to get Noelle and the carrier from the back seat, a cold breeze swirled into the car.

They hurried across the snowy parking lot and into the warm office. Mom checked them in with the receptionist, then they sat on a bench with Noelle in the carrier between them.

The people with dogs sat on the benches on the other side of the desk. One of the dogs whined when he saw Noelle, and another barked and jumped up and down.

"Don't worry, Noelle," Abby whispered into the carrier. "We'll keep you safe from those dogs."

She checked to see if Noelle was nervous, but the cat still laid with her paws tucked under her. Her ears twitched, but she didn't look scared. She just looked annoyed.

There was only one other person with a cat sitting on their side. Their cat looked just as unhappy about being there as Noelle did.

Abby looked at all the animal pictures on the wall while they waited. After a few minutes, a young man came through a door from the back.

"Noelle," he announced.

"Right here," Mom said.

Abby stood at the same time and followed as Mom took the carrier into the examination room.

Once the carrier was on the silver exam table, the man leaned over and looked at Noelle.

"You're a very pretty cat," he said. "And, how perfect that you have a Christmas name when it's the Christmas season."

He straightened. "Dr. Gustafson will be right in. Good luck with Noelle."

"Thank you," Abby and her mother said at the same time.

The man had only been gone for a minute when Dr. Gustafson came in.

"Good afternoon," she said to Mom and Abby. Then she smiled and looked in the carrier. "And hello to you, kitty."

Noelle stared back at her. Dr. Gustafson took her out and set her on the table, petting her with both hands.

"So, I understand Noelle is new to your family," Dr. Gustafson said, looking at Abby.

"Yes. I found her in our barn. We put up posters and called people to see if anyone was missing her, but no one was. I think she picked us to be her family."

Dr. Gustafson smiled and nodded. "Sometimes kitties just know who will love them."

"I do love her already," Abby said.

"Then she's a very lucky kitty," the vet said.

She moved her hands all over Noelle's sides, back, stomach and face. Next, she used a little flashlight to check the cat's eyes, ears, and mouth before checking her abdomen one more time.

"She looks young," the doctor said. "How long has she been with you?"

"About three weeks," Mom answered.

Dr. Gustafson nodded again and scooped up Noelle. "I just have one test I want to do on her in a different exam room. We'll be right back."

Abby stiffened. "Is she okay?"

"Oh, yes, she seems quite healthy," Dr Gustafson said. "How's her appetite?"

"She's been eating a lot," Abby said.

Dr. Gustafson smiled the same warm way she had when she first came into the room.

"I'm sure she has," she said.

Dr. Gustafson hugged Noelle to her chest and opened the door. "This will only take a few minutes. I'll also check to see if she has been microchipped."

"What does that mean?" Abby asked.

Dr. Gustafson pointed at the back of Noelle's neck. "Sometimes owners have a tiny chip put in under the cat's skin right here so, if it gets lost, a vet can check to see who owns it. I'll let you know if she has one."

Abby watched them leave as Mom sank onto the bench in the corner. She leaned back against the wall with her eyes closed, shaking her head.

"Are you worried, Mom?"

Mom smiled but didn't open her eyes. "Not about Noelle," she said. "I'm pretty sure I know what kind of test the vet is doing."

Abby widened her eyes. "It won't hurt Noelle, will it?"

"Not if I'm right," Mom said. "Let's wait and see."

It was less than ten minutes before Dr. Gustafson returned with Noelle. She put her into the carrier and closed the doors, then turned to Abby and her mom.

"First, Noelle has no microchip, so I guess she's now yours," Dr. Gustafson said.

Abby glanced at her mom, who had a funny smile.

"Second," Dr Gustafson said, "my suspicions were correct."

Mom groaned. "She's having kittens, isn't she?"

Abby's head whipped back and forth between Dr. Gustafson and her mom.

"Kittens? Noelle's going to have kittens?" Excitement bubbled in her stomach.

"Yes, she is," Dr. Gustafson said. "The best I can tell from the ultrasound is there are four heartbeats and little skeletons."

"Four kittens?" Abby pressed her hands together. She wanted to clap and jump up and down, but Mom didn't look as excited.

"You'll need to give Noelle a safe and warm place to have her babies," Dr. Gustafson said. "And she won't be able to have her vaccines until the kittens no longer need her."

Abby looked at Noelle then her mom. "Noelle can't live in the garage anymore. It's too cold for kittens."

"Abby," Mom said, looking stern, "I don't know if Noelle will get along with our other cats."

"I can give you ideas for the best way for Noelle to meet them," Dr. Gustafson said. "Maybe then it will be okay."

Abby pressed her palms together like she was praying. "Please, Mom. Since Noelle adopted me, I have to take good care of her and her kittens."

Her mom shook her head and sighed.

"I don't know, Abby. That may be more than we can take on."

Chapter 9

THE INTRODUCTION

When they arrived home, Abby and her mom followed Dr. Gustafson's instructions. They set up Mollie's big gate between the hall and laundry room to separate Noelle from the rest of the house. Next, they put a rug on the floor and set out bowls of food and water so Noelle would have what she needed. Mom found a large foil pan to use as a temporary litter box.

"This looks good," Mom said. "Now let me bring in Noelle."

Mom brought the cat carrier in from the car and set it against the wall.

"Dr. Gustafson suggested we leave the carrier here so Noelle feels she has a safe place to be," Mom said.

She opened the door, and Noelle sauntered from the crate like she wasn't afraid of anything. Abby kneeled next to her to stroke her back.

"You know you're safe here, don't you, Noelle? We'll take good care of you and your kittens."

Suddenly, the sound of Chara and Tanner running made Noelle scurry toward the carrier. They ran so fast that they skidded on the floor when they came around the corner and saw Noelle.

"Whoa!" Abby said, holding up her hand even though she was on the other side of the gate from them. They sniffed the bars and tried to see around Abby to Noelle.

Noelle hissed and cowered against the side of the carrier. Chara turned and ran away, but Tanner took a few steps back, then stopped to stare at Noelle. He hunched his back and flicked his tail back and forth.

"It's okay, Tanner," Abby said, trying to coax him closer to the cage. "You can be friends."

Tanner flattened his ears and growled as he backed away in slow motion.

Noelle's fur and tail puffed up.

"Rrorowww!" She yowled and arched her back.

"Hissss!" Tanner narrowed his eyes, then slinked farther away. He laid down at the edge of the kitchen floor where he could still see Noelle.

"Oh, no!" Abby cried. "They don't like each other."

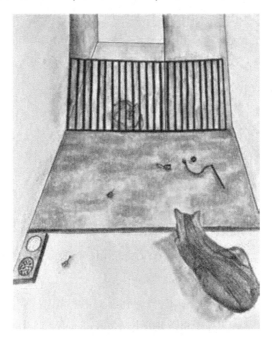

Mom stood. "It takes time, Abby. This is Tanner and Chara's home. They need to get used to another cat being here, and Noelle will need time to get to know them."

"But we can't make Noelle sleep in the garage, anymore," Abby said, "and, I don't want Chara and Tanner to be angry. What do we do?"

"We leave them alone," Mom said, putting her hand on Abby's shoulder. "Noelle is safe behind the gate. We know she and Mollie are friends, so I'm sure it will work out with Chara and Tanner, too. Come on."

Mom opened the gate so she and Abby could leave Noelle's area.

"Abby," Ryan called from the living room, "let's build something with my LEGOS."

Abby stepped past the opening but turned to squat, facing Noelle. She held her hand against the gate. Noelle came to her and rubbed her furry cheek against Abby's palm.

"I'll be back to check on you later," Abby promised.

It was hard to leave Noelle, but Abby pulled herself away. Tanner still laid in the same spot a few feet away, not taking his eyes off Noelle.

On her way, Abby bent to pet him. "Please be friends, Tanner." She left him to watch Noelle, hoping she wouldn't hear a lot of growling and yowling during the night.

The next morning when Abby came downstairs to check on Noelle, Tanner and Chara sat outside the gate grooming themselves. There was no growling. No yowling. No hissing.

Noelle laid on the other side of the gate, seeming to not care that they were there. Abby was relieved and encouraged. There was hope for a friendship among the cats, and if not a friendship, at least tolerance.

"Mom!" Abby called, "it looks like the kitties are getting friendly."

Mom poked her head around the corner. "I noticed. We can probably let Noelle come out when you get home from school," she said. "Noelle seems to especially like you, so I think she'll feel safer if you're here when she explores."

"I'll get her fresh food and water and clean her litter box before I get dressed," Abby said. "She's my cat, and I have to take care of her."

Mom smiled. "You've been very responsible with her, Abby. I'm sure she feels very loved."

After Abby was ready for school, she stopped to check on Noelle once more. Now Chara and Tanner were lying down next to the gate, their noses pushed between the narrow bars.

"Good kitties," she said, petting Chara and Tanner. "We'll see how the three of you do this afternoon."

"Bus is here!" Ryan announced as he ran past them and threw open the door to the garage.

Abby grabbed her backpack from beside the door and hurried out behind him. Before closing the door, she looked back one more time and crossed her fingers. She hoped that would bring good luck that everything would work out when the cats were loose together in the house.

That afternoon, when the bus stopped at the end of their driveway, Abby raced off as fast as she could, with Ryan right behind her. She rushed into the house, eager to see if the cats were getting along.

When she opened the door, Noelle was still behind the gate, but Chara and Tanner were no longer there. Oh no! Did that mean they didn't like each other?

Abby tossed her backpack on the floor and opened the gate to go in with Noelle.

"Hi, Noelle. Are you ready to see the rest of the house?"

"Meow!" Noelle said as she rubbed against Abby's legs.

"Mom?" Abby called. "Can we let Noelle out, now?"

"Sure," Mom called back. "There were no problems all day."

Abby took a big breath, then took down the gate. She hoped this worked. Noelle trotted out of the area and toward the kitchen.

"Here she comes," Abby called. Ryan had already sat down at the table to eat the snack Mom had left for them.

When Noelle walked into the living room, Chara and Tanner both stood up on the cat tree where they'd been sleeping. Their eyes grew big as they watched Noelle sniff the furniture. She moved on to the small box of cat toys and sniffed all of those. When she spotted a small stuffed mouse on the floor by the coffee table, she crouched down, wiggled her backside, then pounced on it. She rolled with it between her paws, biting and kicking it.

Mollie came off her bed in the corner and watched. Then, Chara and Tanner climbed down from their cat tree and peeked from behind the chair.

After a minute, Noelle jumped up and explored more. She sniffed everything in the living room before she moved to the next room.

Mollie followed, and Tanner followed, and Chara followed, and Abby was behind all of them. Abby was relieved that they were interested in Noelle and not growling.

Abby laughed. "It's like we have a parade with Noelle as the leader."

Ryan ran from the kitchen and stepped in line behind Abby. He lifted his knees high like he was marching. "Now it's a longer parade," he said, laughing.

Noelle led them through every room as she explored. Sometimes she stopped suddenly and everyone behind her almost bumped into each other.

Finally, she went back to the living room. She climbed up the cat tree to the very top perch and stared at everyone who had followed her. Mollie laid on her bed where she could still see Noelle.

Chara and Tanner sat on the floor below her, looking up.

Ryan pointed at Noelle and laughed again. "Look! She thinks she's the Lion Queen."

Abby rolled her eyes and laughed, too. "The Lion Queen?" she repeated. "Oh, brother!"

After a minute Mom came into the living room. "How's it going?" she asked.

Abby smiled as she sat in the chair near the cat tree. "I think everything's going to be just fine," she said.

Mom crossed the room to Noelle and put a big holiday bow next to her. "Merry early Christmas, Abby. Noelle is your first gift."

Warmth started in Abby's middle and spread through her body.

"Noelle's a perfect present," Abby said, getting up to scratch Noelle under the chin. "And, having a home is a Christmas present for Noelle,"

Noelle purred and rolled over on her back so Abby could rub her belly.

Mom smiled. "And it looks like Noelle agrees."

Ryan ran to the Christmas tree in the corner of the room and plugged in the lights. They sparkled to life and lit up the room.

"Merry Christmas, everyone!"

Chapter 10

MOVING IN

That night when Abby was reading in bed, Noelle jumped up next to her. She kneaded her paws in the green blanket and purred as she rubbed her cheek against Abby's arm.

"Meow!" Noelle said.

"Are you happy you found a safe home?" Abby asked.

"Meow!" Noelle answered, then nudged Abby's arm and book out of the way so she could climb on her lap.

Abby laughed. "I guess that means yes." She hugged her new cat, then started to read out loud so Noelle could hear the story, too.

Later, when Mom and Dad came to tuck her in, Mollie, Chara, and Tanner came in, too. Mollie sat next to the bed and stared at Noelle. Chara and Tanner jumped onto the bed and curled up together at the end where they always slept.

"This looks like a pet party," Dad said as he bent to kiss Abby on the forehead.

"I'm so happy all of the animals get along," Abby said. "I know it was a hard decision to have another cat, but I feel like we saved Noelle and her kittens."

"Yes, you're probably right," Mom said. She patted Noelle's head. "She even looks like she's smiling."

"I think she is," Abby said. "I'm giving her love and making her feel safe. Maybe she never felt that before."

Dad stepped to the door but then turned around.

"We're proud of how responsible you are, Abby," he said. "Noelle deserves to feel safe and loved just like Chara, Tanner, and Mollie. We'll make this work."

Mollie thumped her tail against the floor when Dad said her name.

Abby snuggled Noelle. "All animals deserve to feel that way. I can't wait for her to have her kittens, so we can love them, too."

Mom's expression turned serious. "Just remember, we have to find homes for her kittens. Seven cats are too many for us."

Abby suddenly felt sad. "But nobody else could love them like Noelle and I will."

"Yes, they will," Mom said. "We'll find perfect homes for them where they'll be safe and loved, just like here. We'll take very good care of them until then."

Abby didn't want to think about that, now. Instead, she'd imagine what it was going to be like to have little kittens racing around the house.

"Good night, Sweetie," Mom said. "Fifteen more minutes of reading, then it's lights out. Sweet dreams."

"Good night," Abby said. "I love you."

"I love you, too," Mom said as she slipped from the room.

Every night after that, Noelle slept on Abby's bed just like Chara and Tanner. Then, each morning, when Abby got out of bed, there was a cat parade behind her as she went down the stairs to feed them. She felt more grown up with this new responsibility.

A week later, on Christmas morning, Abby woke to find all the cats off her bed. She rolled from under the covers and ran to the top of the stairs where Ryan was already sitting.

"It's Christmas morning!" he said, jumping up. "Mom said I couldn't wake you up, but now you're up. We can go down for presents."

"I don't know where the cats are," Abby said. She couldn't even think about presents until she'd taken care of them.

"Mom already took them down to feed them." He grabbed her hand. "Let's go!"

They pounded down the stairs and ran into the living room. The lights on the tree sparkled, making little dots of light on the walls around it. Presents were neatly laid out underneath it, and on top of them were two stockings stuffed with goodies.

"Merry Christmas!" Mom and Dad said together as they came into the living room.

"It's finally Christmas!" Ryan said again, plopping onto the floor next to the tree. "Let's open presents!"

Abby hugged her parents then sat cross legged on the floor by Ryan. There was one big package under the tree that hadn't been there the night before. She leaned forward to look at the tag.

TO: ABBY

FROM: DAD

She twisted to look at her father. "What's this?" she asked.

Dad sat in his chair and sipped from the steaming cup of coffee he'd carried in. "Something special. Save it to open last," he said with a wink.

Mom sat on the couch, and Chara and Tanner jumped up next to her.

Abby moved to her knees and glanced around the room. "Where's Noelle?" She felt her heartbeat speed up.

"She's still eating breakfast," Mom explained. "She has to eat enough for babies, too."

Abby noticed in the last couple of days that Noelle was getting plumper. She wondered how big the babies were now.

"Do you think she'll have her kittens soon?" Abby asked.

Mom smiled. "They won't be Christmas babies, if that's what you're thinking. I think it will be within a couple of weeks, though."

"Are we going to open presents, or not?" Ryan asked.

"You can hand them out this year, Ryan, but leave the big one for Abby for last," Mom said.

Ryan darted from Dad, to Abby, to Mom, to the place where he set his own gifts. When all the gifts were given out and opened, all attention turned to the big package under the tree.

Dad rose from the chair and went to the tree. He slid the big package out to the middle of the floor.

"I made this special for you, Abby," Dad said.

Abby and Ryan scooted closer.

Abby laid her hand on the shiny wrapping paper, then looked up at Dad. "Really? You made it for me?"

Dad laughed. "Well, yes and no. You'll see what I mean when you open it."

"I can't wait to see what it is," Ryan said, pushing it closer to Abby. "It's heavy. Hurry! Open it." He bounced on his knees while he waited.

Abby took hold of a corner of the paper and tugged. Then another piece. And another.

Ryan reached his hand out to grab a corner, too.

"Ryan!" Mom said. "Let Abby open it."

"It's okay," Abby said, looking up at her brother, "you can help me open it."

Ryan snagged a piece of the wrapping paper while Abby peeled back a large area. She peeked at the part that was visible. It was something made of wood.

She remembered hearing her father sawing and hammering in the basement recently, but he often made things. Now she knew all that noise was because he was making something for her.

Two more pulls of paper from Abby and Ryan, and the gift was revealed.

"Wow! Is this for Noelle to have her kittens in?" Abby asked.

It was a beautiful wooden box with a cat bed inside. She ran her hand along the soft material.

"It is," Dad said. "I know you were going to set up a cardboard box, but I thought a solid box of her own would be nice."

Abby jumped up and wrapped her arms around her dad's waist. "This is awesome, Dad. Thank you! I'm sure she'll love it."

At that moment, Noelle strolled into the room, dodging the strips and wads of paper that had been tossed to the side.

"Noelle, come here, kitty," Abby said, patting the inside of the box. "This is for you."

Noelle sniffed along the entire edge until she had circled the box. She lifted one front paw and carefully touched the bed inside, then sniffed that, too. Finally, she hopped over the edge, circled three times on the cushion, then curled up inside the box. She looked up at Abby and blinked slowly. Abby knew from her cat care books that it meant Noelle was happy.

"Aww, she's purring," Abby said, petting her. "She loves it, Dad. This will be the perfect place for her to have her babies. This is the best present ever."

"And it's not even for you," Ryan added, laughing. "You can't sleep in there."

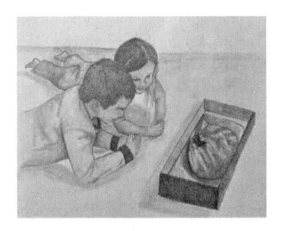

"We'll put it in the pantry," Mom said. "That way we can close the door so we know where she is, but she can still see out through the window. Cats often hide to have their kittens, so we'll make that her special place."

Abby nodded. "I'll move it there after she gets out of it."

Mom stood. "That's a good plan. Let's have breakfast and let mama kitty sleep and get used to her new bed."

Abby's stomach growled. She was ready for mom's big Christmas breakfast. She started to follow the others out of the room, then went back to stroke the top of Noelle's head.

"You're lucky you found us, Noelle, and your kittens will be lucky, too."

Chapter 11

THEN THERE WERE SEVEN

Every morning starting the day after Christmas, Abby jumped out of bed and ran downstairs to see if the kittens had been born. But, for two weeks, she opened the door and saw only Noelle.

It was a Saturday morning when Abby went to the pantry to check and found Chara and Tanner lying outside the door. Their noses were pressed against the small opening at the bottom.

"What are you two nosey-roseys doing?" She kneeled and petted them both. "Can I check on Noelle?" she asked. "I bet you all want your breakfast."

She slowly opened the door, expecting Noelle to burst from the small room like she did every morning. But, this time, the cat wasn't waiting to escape.

"Noelle," she called, peeking around the door.

Then she gasped and covered her mouth.

Snuggled next to Noelle were four little furballs. There was a gray, a black, and two gray-striped kittens.

"Oh, my goodness!" she whispered even though she wanted to shout. "You had your babies. You're a mommy, Noelle."

"Mom! Dad!" Abby whispered out the door. "Noelle had her kittens."

Mom and Dad tiptoed down the hall and looked in at Noelle and her sleeping kittens. The babies made little squeaking noises as they snuggled in as close to their mommy as they could.

Abby took a step closer to Noelle's box, but Mom put a hand on her shoulder to stop her.

"That's close enough," Mom said. "Sometimes mama kitties prefer to be left alone when they have newborns. They're protective of their babies."

Abby leaned over to look a little closer. She could see that their eyes were closed tight.

"They can't see," Abby said, worried.

"That's how kittens are when they're born," Mom said, "but in a week or a little after that, their eyes will open. After that, they'll grow fast and will run around and play. We'll have to kitten proof our house."

Abby bent to look even closer to inspect the kittens' faces. "I read in the book from the library that cats are the only animals born with whiskers. And look, you can see them."

"I never knew that," Mom said. "That's very interesting. You learned a lot from reading that book."

"I did," Abby said proudly.

Mollie, Chara, and Tanner peeked around the door, too. Abby was sure they would all be friends, too.

She heard Ryan's feet pounding on the floor, then he slid to a stop just outside the door.

"Let me see!" He squeezed in next to Abby and poked his head around the door. "They're so little!" he exclaimed.

"Shh!" Abby scolded, holding her finger up to her lips. "We don't want to scare them."

Ryan's finger bounced in the air as he counted the kittens from a distance. "Four?" he whispered.

Abby nodded. "We have seven cats now."

"Two kittens for each of us," he said. "Which ones do you want to be yours?"

"Oh, no, no, no!" Mom said before Abby could answer. "We're going to find good homes for these kittens when they're old enough."

Abby's shoulders dropped. "I know. Can we pet them?"

Mom put her hand on Abby's and Ryan's arms. "Let's leave Noelle and her babies alone to rest," she said. "Abby, you can make sure she has food and water and her litter box is cleaned, but let's give them time to adjust. Tomorrow, we'll see if Noelle will let us pet and hold them."

"I love them already," Abby said, backing away from the door.

"I'm sure you'll have fun with them as they grow," Dad said, "as long as you remember that you'll raise them to be wonderful pets for someone else."

A lump clogged Abby's throat. She couldn't imagine giving them away. She was glad it would be a long time before she had to think about that.

It was hard for Abby to stay out of the room where Noelle and the kittens were. The next night, when her mom agreed, she and Ryan had their first chance to hold them.

"We're going to put a gate across the door," Mom said. "I want Chara, Tanner, and Mollie to get used to seeing and hearing the kittens, but I want Noelle to feel they're safe."

As soon as Abby opened the door, Noelle ran from the pantry. "You don't like being locked in, do you Noelle?" she said. "You'll be able to jump over the gate whenever you want to now."

The kittens squeaked and squirmed as soon as Noelle left the bed. They crawled around on their bellies, unable to lift their heads.

"Mew! Mew! Mew!"

Their tiny little voices joined together to make a loud, piercing noise.

Abby covered her ears and tiptoed into the room, worried about frightening the kittens.

"Shh! Shh! It's okay babies," she said in the softest voice she could use.

She sat on the floor next to the bed.

"Mew! Mew! Mew! Mew!"

The kittens piled together, crawling over each other like a bunch of worms, squeaking and squealing for their mother.

Abby reached in and picked up one of the gray striped ones from the top. She cupped it in her hands and snuggled it under her chin. The soft fur tickled her skin there.

"Hello, little baby," she cooed. The kitten cried while it wriggled in her hands. The high-pitched sound made Abby's ears ring.

Suddenly, Noelle launched herself back over the gate and pushed her nose against the kitten in Abby's hands. She used her teeth to grab the back of the baby's neck.

"Noelle, don't bite your baby," Abby said, pulling the kitten out of Noelle's reach.

"She's not biting her," Mom said from the other side of the gate. Abby hadn't heard her mom move closer. "Mother cats carry their babies by the scruff of their neck. To us it looks like they're hurting them, but the kittens go limp and let their mom carry them.

Noelle is telling you that she wants her baby back in the bed. Put her back with the others."

"Noelle doesn't trust me?" Abby asked, disappointed. She placed the kitten back with its siblings.

"It's instinct, Abby. Her job is to protect her babies, and if they're crying, she wants to be near them."

As if she heard Mom, Noelle hopped back in the box and stretched out in front of the kittens. They squirmed over each other again so they could get to her belly for milk. They used their tiny paws to press against her belly and rub their noses along Noelle's fur. When they found a spot to drink, they squeaked.

Abby giggled. "They sound like they need to be oiled."

"They're happy," Mom said. "You'll see that they'll grow fast on their mama's milk."

Noelle kneaded the bed with her paws while the kittens ate. Her purring was loud in the small room.

"I can't wait until they're big enough to play," Abby said. She stood and climbed on the other side of the gate. She looked back at their little bodies that fit in the palm of her hands. It was hard to be patient with such furry cuteness so close.

Chapter 12

HIDING PLACES

After only two weeks, all four kittens' eyes were open. They waddled when they walked, sometimes toppling over if they tried to run. They were still little balls of fluff with legs.

"You silly kittens," Abby said as she picked them up one at a time to snuggle. She had already learned their personalities.

The gray one, a girl, was brave and tried to climb out of the box. One time she was successful at climbing over the edge, but then flopped over when she dropped onto the floor.

The bigger gray-striped one, another girl, liked to climb all over the others. One time she climbed on Noelle and laid on her head like a fur hat.

The smaller gray striped kitten was a girl, too. She was shy. When Abby reached in to pick her up, she squealed, squeaked, and mewed until Abby set her back in the box.

The black kitten was the only boy. When Abby picked him up, he snuggled into her neck. She gently hugged him.

"I wish I could give you a name," she said, "but Mom said we should let your new families name you."

The little kitten mewed like he was talking.

"You know what? I'll call you B.K. for black kitty," she said.

While she snuggled him, she looked at the others. That's what she would do. She'd give them each initials so it wasn't real names. The gray kitten would be G.G. for gray girl. The shy kitten would be S.K. for shy kitty.

Abby set B.K. back into the box and picked up the bigger striped kitten. "What do I call you?" she asked, turning the kitten so she could look into her face.

"I know," she said, giggling. "I'm going to call you K.K. for kitty kitty."

She stroked the kitten's back. She tried not to think about them going to new homes, but she knew they would when they were old enough. For now, she'd give them plenty of attention, so they'd know she loved them.

The garage door slammed, then Ryan stopped at the gate. His cheeks were rosy from being outside.

"Can I come in, too?" he asked. He yanked off his gloves, tossed his hat onto the floor and shrugged out of his coat. "I'll pick those up later. I want to hold the kittens."

He hopped over the gate, then sat on the floor next to Abby.

"I gave them all initials so we know who we're talking about." She pointed at each kitten as she shared their temporary names.

"I want to hold B.K. We're both boys, so we have to stick together," he said, reaching past Abby to pick up the black kitten. B.K. flopped in Ryan's and squealed until Ryan pressed him against his chest. "See, he likes me. He's not crying anymore."

Abby didn't have a favorite. She loved them all and wished none of them ever had to leave.

The kittens were three weeks old when they disappeared. Abby played with them after school, then when they were sleepy, she laid them back in the box and went outside with Ryan to go sledding on the hill behind the barn.

When their hands and feet tingled from the cold, they came back inside. Abby tucked her mittens in her pockets, then hung her coat and snow pants on the hook in the laundry room.

"I'll make your hot cocoa, now," Mom said, coming in from the living room. She set the blanket she was knitting on the counter before taking two cups from the cupboard.

"Did you have fun?" she asked. She filled the cups with milk and cocoa mix, then put them in the microwave to heat.

"There's good snow on the hill," Abby said. "It's packed down, so we were able to go really fast."

"Yeah, and we went really far, too," Ryan said as he slid onto a chair at the table to wait for his hot cocoa.

Abby walked down the hall toward the pantry. "I'm going to check to see if the kittens are awake."

When she got to the gate, she leaned over it to look around the door. Her body tensed when she saw Noelle's box.

It was empty.

She quickly moved the gate so she could go into the small room. Where could the kittens go? Even Noelle was gone.

"Mom?" she yelled, whirling around to look at the shelves that held packages of paper towels and canned goods. No kittens. "Mom?" she yelled again, panic making her voice go higher.

"Abby, what's wrong?" her mother asked, hurrying to the doorway.

"Noelle and the kittens have disappeared!"

"Disappeared?" Mom repeated. She looked into the room, but there was nowhere for a full-grown cat and kittens to hide.

Ryan ran to the door. "They're gone?" he asked. "Someone stole them?"

Mom put her hand on top of his head. "No, no one stole them."

Goosebumps jumped out on Abby's skin. She was supposed to take care of the kittens, and now while she was sledding, they had disappeared.

"What do we do?" she asked, hurrying into the kitchen.

The timer on the microwave went off as she went by. She couldn't even think about hot cocoa right now.

"Abby, calm down," Mom said. "I'm sure I know what happened to the kittens."

Abby spun to look at her mother. "What?"

"Noelle probably moved them."

"Moved them? Where?" Abby looked all around the kitchen. "I thought she loved the bed Dad made for her and the kittens."

"I don't know where," Mom said, "but it's not unusual for mama cats to decide they want their kittens in a safer place. Noelle probably found a hiding spot somewhere in the house."

"But they were safe in the pantry," Abby exclaimed, throwing her hands in the air.

"Cats don't think like we do," Mom said as she stirred the two mugs of hot cocoa. "Noelle will come out to eat, and when she does, we'll watch where she goes after just to make sure where she hid them is a safe spot."

Mom handed Abby a mug of cocoa and carried Ryan's to the table.

"Are you sure?" Abby asked.

"I'm sure," Mom said. Ryan took the cocoa, tossed five mini marshmallows in his then pushed the bag to Abby.

Abby added marshmallows, thinking about all the things she was learning about cats and kittens that she hadn't read in the cat care book from the library. Did Noelle move them because Abby wasn't doing a good enough job taking care of them?

Just before dinner, Abby took a can of cat food from the cupboard and tapped the top with a spoon. As always, Chara and Tanner charged into the hall and stood at their bowls, waiting. Abby kept tapping, watching for Noelle.

Then she heard the soft footsteps on the basement stairs, and Noelle came through the partially open door.

"Noelle, there you are," she said as she put a spoon of moist cat food in each cat's bowl. "Where did you hide your kittens?"

Noelle rubbed against Abby's legs and purred before going to her bowl.

While the cats ate, Abby went to the living room where her mom and dad were watching the news.

"Noelle came out to eat," Abby told her. "She came from the basement."

Her mom rose from the couch. "Let's get a couple of flashlights and do a quick search," she said. "Make sure you stop and just listen, too. You might hear something before you see them."

Ryan, who had been playing on the floor with his trucks, popped up.

"Can I help, too?" he asked. I wanna find B.K."

"I want to find *all* of them," Abby said on her way to the kitchen to get flashlights.

Even though the lights in the basement were on, they used their flashlights to look behind boxes, under the deck furniture stored in the basement for the winter, and around the shelves of tools and nails. Nothing.

Abby crept around the corner near the workbench. She froze when she thought she heard something.

"Mew! Mew! Mew!"

Tiny kitten voices were coming from somewhere near the shelf. She carefully pushed aside some boxes stacked there. Then her light reflected off little eyes. The kittens cried even louder.

"I found them!" Abby called to her mother and Ryan. "Isn't it too cold down here for them?"

Her mom and Ryan joined her and used their flashlights to peek in at the kittens.

"Let's bring the blanket down for them," she said. "Hopefully Noelle will be okay with that and won't move them again."

"Mew! Mew! Mew!" the kittens cried, and moments later, they heard Noelle running down the basement stairs.

"Let's leave them alone," Mom said, "or Noelle might move them again. At least right now we know where they are."

They hurried away from the area, hoping Noelle wouldn't see them near the kittens.

Over the next two weeks, it became a game of hide and seek. Noelle moved the kittens three more times. One time Abby found them inside the back of the old recliner in the basement. Then, Noelle moved the kittens to the bottom of the linen closet in the upstairs bathroom. The last time she hid them, Abby found them back in the basement in the first hiding space on the shelf.

By then, the kittens were much more active, and even Noelle couldn't keep them in one place.

"It's time to move them back to the pantry," Mom said one day. "We'll give them cat toys to keep them busy and set up baby gates so they can't get out. There are too many things for them to get into if they roam the whole house."

Abby carried K.K., her mom carried S.K. and G.G., and Ryan carried B.K. They set them over the gate, and the kittens scurried to the toys. Two climbed the scratching post, racing to see who would get to the top first. One played with the ball in the plastic ring, and another played with a furry stuffed mouse.

Mom grabbed the other two gates that were leaning against the wall.

"We'll put up the gates three high," Mom said as she snapped them into place in the doorway. "We don't want these little mischief-makers to get out of here."

When she was finished, Abby tugged on each one to make sure they were secure.

"What about Noelle?" Abby asked. "She can't get to them."

"We'll let her in with them as soon as she wants," Mom said. "They're getting old enough that she'll want breaks from them anyway."

Abby shook the gate one more time. There were so many things kittens could get into and be hurt. Would this keep them safe?

Chapter 13

OUTSMARTING THE KITTENS

Every day after school, Abby took the gates down, and she and Ryan played with the kittens in the living room. As always, B.K. climbed all over Ryan as if they were best friends. The other kittens raced from end to end, scrambling across furniture and darting around the coffee table legs.

Keeping up with them was difficult. One kitten raced up the curtain. Another kitten grabbed her shoestrings and untied her shoes just as she ran to get another kitten off the shelf where it knocked over every photo frame on it.

"Whew! These kittens are busy," Abby said as she put the kitten on the floor and reset the frames.

Ryan dangled a feather toy at the end of the cat tunnel, and B.K. ran through as G.G. jumped and landed on his hand.

He laughed as he rolled away. "There are kittens everywhere!"

Noelle stretched out on the couch sleeping, one eyelid occasionally lifting to check on the antics. Mollie watched from the floor at the end of the couch, her ears lifted so she wouldn't miss a move the kittens made.

The tiger kittens rolled and wrestled, tumbling until they hit Mollie's paw. She poked them with her nose, and they scrambled to their feet and ran over her body and onto the couch to get to the safety of their mother.

"What's going on in here?" Mom asked when she walked in. "It sounds like a herd of elephants running through."

Abby sat on the floor with her legs stretched out in front of her. "It's just these crazy kittens." She picked up B.K. and hugged him, but he kicked and squirmed until she put him back down. With his tail straight up in the air, he shot across the room and launched himself onto the loveseat, then circled around and raced back across the floor, slamming into G.G., causing her to roll to her side.

"They have so much energy," Abby said, grabbing another toy for them to play with. Two kittens pounced on it.

"I came in to tell you that friends of mine will be here in a few minutes to see the kittens," Mom said. "They're interested in adopting the gray kitten."

Abby twisted to look at her mom. "G.G.?"

Her mom lifted her eyebrows.

"G.G.?" she questioned. "Remember we decided to let the families name the kittens?"

Abby nodded. "It's just initials. G.G. stands for gray girl. I needed to call them something other than kitty 1, 2, 3, and 4."

Mom smiled. "Okay, as long as you're not getting too attached. It will be hard enough to let them go when it's time. Using the names the families give them will make it easier."

"I know," Abby said, stroking G.G.'s back.

Mom left the room, and Abby and Ryan went back to playing with the kittens. By the time the friends arrived, the kittens had worn themselves out and were snuggled into a pile near the scratching post.

When they came in, Abby took the gray kitten from the furry pile and handed her to the woman while the man watched, smiling. The woman hugged the kitten, then she sat in the chair and let the kitten curl up on her lap.

"We've decided to name her Grace," the woman said. "We're going to love her so much. We have a bed, and toys, and everything she needs for when we adopt her. We're very excited."

Grace woke up and stretched her front legs out. The man kneeled and gently stroked her paws. "She'll be perfect," he said. He looked at Abby. "We loved our last cat, but she was old and passed away last year. We miss her very much, so Grace will fill the hole in our hearts."

Abby smiled as she watched them cuddle Grace. These people were going to love Grace just as much as she did. Knowing that she would be going to such a loving home made it easier to think about letting her go.

"It will be a few more weeks before they'll be old enough to leave," Mom told them, "but you can visit her anytime. We know she'll have a very happy life with you."

"You can be sure of it," the woman said. "We're in love already."

Two days later, Abby was playing with the kittens again when her mother told her about the families who wanted to adopt the black one and the two gray striped ones.

"The black kitten will be adopted by a young woman who is an artist," Mom explained. "She's naming him Bob after her favorite artist. The two tiger kittens are being adopted together. The family has had some sad things happen recently, and they hope having the kittens will make them smile again. They're naming them Stormy and Sky Dancer."

Abby's chest tightened. Even though she knew the kittens were going to new homes, when they were unnamed, it was easy to pretend they were staying. Names made their eventual departure real.

"Aw, those are cute names," Abby said, pretending to be happy, but the tightness in her voice revealed her true feelings.

"Abby, I know it's hard, but we can't keep the kittens. It costs money for vaccinations, food, and litter boxes. And, if they get sick, they have to go to the veterinarian. If we're going to have animals, then we have to be responsible and take care of them. We can't afford four more."

"I know," Abby said, fighting tears. "Sometimes I just think no one else can love them like I do."

She looked at the kittens who had stopped playing and were lined up like little stuffed animals on a bed.

Mom smiled and hugged Abby. "That's because you've been very responsible in taking care of them and you have a big heart." Mom stepped back and held Abby at the shoulders. "We'll check in on the kittens after they go to their new homes. You'll see how much they'll be loved."

Abby only nodded because the lump in her throat made it hard to breathe. Talking was out of the question. She would miss the kittens when they left, but for now, she'd give them all the love and attention she could.

That night after dinner, Abby and Ryan played with the kittens again to tire them out. Abby noticed again that Bob, the black kitten, always seemed to be with Ryan. Ryan played with the others, too, but it was clear that Bob was his favorite.

When it was time for bed, Abby put each of the kittens over the gate into the pantry. While refilling the food bowl, she heard scrambling behind her. She turned to see Stormy and Grace climbing the only gate set up in the doorway.

"Hey, you two!" She put down the food and grabbed the two kittens before they got over the gate. "It's time for bed. You need to stay here."

She went back to pick up the bag of food. When she turned around to leave, the other two kittens were climbing the gate.

"Bob! Sky Dancer!" she scolded as she took them off the gate and set them in the cat bed. "It's time to go to bed."

She was ready to step over the gate when Grace raced to it and climbed up before Abby could stop her.

"Oh, my goodness!" she said, snagging the kitten before she reached the top. "I have to be like an octopus with eight arms in order to keep you all in here."

Dad stepped up to the door as she put Grace in the bed with two of the other kittens.

"Having some trouble?" he asked, smiling.

"Every time I try to go over the gate, the kittens run and try to get over it before me. Can you help me put the other two gates on top of this so they can't get out?"

"Sure," Dad said, holding his hand out to Abby to help her over before the kittens could scurry to it.

They stacked the gates in the doorway until only a small opening remained at the top.

"There," Dad said, laughing. "That should keep the little monsters in for the night. There's no way they can get out, now."

Abby slapped her palm against her forehead.

"It's getting harder and harder to keep up with them," Abby said. "They're getting very fast."

Dad put his arm around Abby's shoulders as they walked upstairs. "Well, we outsmarted them this time."

Chapter 14

DISASTER

It didn't take Abby long to fall asleep that night. She was exhausted after chasing the kittens around the house as she tried to keep them out of trouble.

She was in the middle of a dream when suddenly a crash woke her. Her heart beat hard against her chest, and her hands shook. Was the crash part of her dream?

Mollie started barking in the hallway at the top of the stairs. Abby heard her parents' bedroom door open.

"You stay up here with the kids," her father said in a loud whisper to her mother. Mollie barked again.

Abby crawled out of bed and tiptoed to her bedroom door. It was already open, so she peeked around the corner. The hall was lit by the nightlight, and she saw her father's back just as he and Mollie started down the stairs.

Mom wrapped the belt to her bathrobe around her waist as she stepped out of her bedroom.

"Mom?" Abby whispered from her doorway. "What's going on? I heard a crash."

Mom motioned for Abby to hurry to her side and pulled her close to her hip.

"We heard it, too," Mom whispered. "Dad's checking to make sure no one broke in, but maybe Mollie's barking scared them away.".

Goosebumps popped up on Abby's arms, and her whole body shook. She was afraid for her dad and Mollie. She was afraid for all of them. With a crash that loud, there could be more than one burglar in the house, and she didn't like to think of her father and Mollie facing them alone.

"Maybe we should call the police," Abby suggested.

"Shh!" her mom said, putting a finger to her lips. "Let's listen."

For a few moments there was no sound. All Abby could hear was her heartbeat in her ears. She glanced at Ryan's bedroom door. She couldn't believe the crash didn't wake him up, too.

The light at the bottom of the stairs came on, faintly lighting the stairway all the way to the top. Abby heard her father's footsteps as he walked through the dining room. Then Abby heard his voice.

"Oh, boy!" he said, then five seconds later, "Oh, boy!"

Abby glanced up at her mother, but her mother only shrugged.

"Is everything okay?" Mom called.

"Come on down," Dad said. "No one broke in, but we do have a little kitten trouble."

Abby glanced up at her mom. "Kitten trouble?" she asked.

"Let's go and see," Mom said.

She led the way down the stairs. Abby followed, both curious and nervous about what trouble they'd find. As soon as Mom turned on the light in the dining room, the problem was obvious.

Mom gasped and covered her mouth with one hand. "Oh, my!"

Abby stepped around her and stared at the mess in front of them.

The tablecloth from the dining room table lay crumpled in a heap on the floor. Water from the broken vase of flowers from Valentine's Day that had been in the middle of the table seeped through the cloth. Five roses were caught in the folds. One rose had been pulled all the way across the floor into the doorway to the kitchen.

"Oh my gosh!" Abby exclaimed. "What a mess!"

"Oh, it doesn't stop here," Dad said. "No rooms were spared. Take a look."

He snapped on the overhead light in the kitchen. Abby continued past him, then stopped. The magnets that held notes on the refrigerator were scattered across the floor. Every note they'd held was either shredded or had bite marks.

She turned and looked in the living room. The dirt from the big potted plant Mom kept by the window had been flung all over the floor. The magazines from the coffee table had been knocked off, and some of the pages were ripped. The same pictures on the shelf that the kittens had knocked over days before were knocked over again.

Abby turned to her dad. "How did this happen?" she asked.

"Go look at the kittens," he said. She couldn't tell if he was annoyed or in shock.

She walked down the hall toward the pantry. As she passed the small bathroom, she saw something white out of the corner of her eye. She reached in and turned on the light. On the floor were piles of shredded toilet paper that had been pulled off the roll. A few squares still hung from the cardboard.

"Oh, no!" she whispered, scrubbing her hands across her face. She couldn't believe what she was seeing. How could four little kittens do this much damage?

With the light on, she also had a full view of the pantry and the gates she and her father had put up. In front of them, all four kittens sat bunched together like they were protecting each other. On the other side of the gates sat Noelle, staring at her naughty kittens.

Abby whirled toward her father. "Did they climb all the way to the top and over the gates?" she asked.

He nodded. "Apparently."

"Now what do we do?" she asked.

"First, we put these kittens back in with their mother, and from now on we close the door when we don't want them to get into mischief. Then," he said pointing back toward the rest of the house, "there's cleaning to do before we go back to bed."

In her head, Abby pictured the messes in all the rooms. She was glad it was the weekend because it would take a long time to clean up. She'd need to catch up on her sleep tomorrow if she was going to keep up with the kittens. Who knew what they'd get into next!

Chapter 15

CHANGES

The bigger the kittens grew, the more trouble they found. One day Sky Dancer disappeared. When Abby searched for her, she eventually found the kitten sleeping, curled up inside Dad's sneaker under the bed.

Another day, the kittens were playing on the cat tree. When Mollie trotted by to go outside with Mom, Grace pounced on her back and rode on her all the way to the door like she was a pony. Mollie turned around in circles trying to reach the kitten, but Grace stayed in place. Abby chased after them and grabbed Grace off Mollie's back in mid-circle.

Bob and Stormy won the prize for causing the biggest problem. Abby was lying on the floor in the living room playing with the other cats when Bob and

Stormy raced into the room – pulling several strands of Mom's pink yarn behind them.

Abby scrambled to her feet and grabbed it from them. Her heart sank as she gathered it, following the lines of yarn through the hall, up the stairs, and into the office where Mom kept all her knitting projects. Several skeins of yarn had been pulled out of Mom's knitting bag and littered the office floor.

"Oh, no!" she cried with her hands on her head.

All four kittens raced into the room and ran through the piles of yarn.

"No, kitties!" Abby said, scooping up the kittens before they could do more damage. She juggled them in her arms. As she snagged each new kitten, she held their furry, wriggling bodies against her chest.

At the same time, Ryan came running up the stairs. "This is a big mess!" he said.

"I know," Abby said. "I read in the cat care book that string and yarn are dangerous for cats, because they could swallow it. I need to clean this up before Mom comes back in from the barn. Can you take a couple of kittens so we can put them in the pantry? They're getting into too much trouble, and I don't want them to be hurt by swallowing the yarn."

Ryan took two from her arms, and they carried them downstairs. Putting them in the pantry was just as tricky. As soon as they'd get three kittens in, two scrambled up and over the gate. Abby felt like a cartoon character with ten arms with her hands going everywhere trying to catch them and put them back.

"Ryan, can you please grab a couple of ping pong balls from their toybox in the living room?" she asked while picking kittens off the gate and setting them back inside the pantry.

"Okay," he said as he jogged down the hall.

"Mew! Mew!" The kittens all cried at once.

"No! You stay there," she ordered. "You've already caused enough mischief for one day." She called down the hall, "Ryan, hurry!"

Ryan's feet pounded on the floor, and in less than a minute he was back.

"Here!" he said, holding out his hands.

Abby took the ping pong balls and tossed them into the small pantry. "Chase these, kitties."

As soon as the balls bounced on the floor, the kittens skittered after them. When the kittens were away from the gate, Abby quickly closed the door.

She leaned her back against the wall and wiped the back of her hand across her forehead. "Whew! Now I have to take care of all of Mom's yarn before she gets back inside."

It took several minutes for Abby to separate the yarn colors. They were no longer in their neat packages. She rolled them into balls so Mom could still easily use them. She was almost finished when she heard her mother coming up the stairs.

Her mom stopped in the doorway and put her hands on her hips.

"Ryan said the kittens have been busy," she said, looking at the balls of yarn Abby had set on the chair. "I guess he was right."

Abby nodded. "They got into your knitting bag." She pointed at the chair. "The yarn isn't like it was in the packages, but I did the best I could."

125

Mom stepped over and picked up a couple of the yarn balls. "These will be fine," she said. "I guess we need to keep the doors closed now that the kittens are so active. I thought it would be a while before they'd be able to climb the stairs." She took a big breath, then turned to go back downstairs. "I'm sure we'll miss all of this craziness when they're gone."

Abby felt the corners of her mouth tugging down. She tried not to think about the kittens leaving, because it always made her sad. She knew that day was coming soon, but the reminders hurt her heart.

After dinner, Abby was reading in her room when the phone rang. She could tell by her mother's part of the conversation that she was talking to someone about one of the kittens. Curious, she laid her book on the bed and ran downstairs. The call was just ending when Abby walked in the kitchen.

"Was that something about the kittens?" Abby asked.

Mom nodded. "The young woman who was going to adopt Bob is changing jobs and doesn't feel it would be fair to him if she adopted him. Her workdays will be too long, and kittens need attention."

"So, he's not leaving?" Abby asked. Excitement flickered in her stomach.

"Not with her," Mom said, "but we'll find him a different home."

Abby didn't know whether to feel happy or sad. For now, Bob was staying with them. But for how long?

"If she's not adopting him, I guess he's not Bob, now," Abby said.

Mom laughed. "Not Bob? That's a funny name for a kitten."

"I'll start calling him N.B. for Not Bob," Abby explained. Suddenly she thought of her cousin whose initials were C.B. Lots of times Abby called her Ceebs. All she had to do was change the first letter.

"Neebs!" she exclaimed. "C.B. is Ceebs, and N.B. can be Neebs."

Nodding, Mom said, "That's a cute name."

"I bet there's no other cat anywhere in the world with that name," Abby said.

"Well, that will work until we find a new family for him and they decide on his final name."

Abby shrugged. "Maybe they'll like it so much that they'll keep it."

"I guess we'll have to see when we find him a new family," Mom said. "The kittens will be ready to go to their new homes in a couple of weeks."

Abby frowned. "Already?"

"Yes, already. I'm taking them back to Dr. Gustafson tomorrow for their checkups and first shots," Mom explained. "A couple of weeks after that, they'll be old enough to go."

"I don't think I'm ready," Abby said.

Mom hugged Abby. "We'll never be ready, but we don't want the kittens to get too settled here and then have to readjust to a new home. This is the best thing for them."

Abby wrapped her arms tighter around her mom. She wondered if Noelle would be sad when her kittens left. It was impossible to imagine them somewhere else.

She pushed the thought from her head. Her mom had been very careful about choosing the kittens' new families. She told Abby that she had gone to the new homes to make sure they would be safe and well taken care of. Even though it was hard, Abby had to trust that these people would give the kittens wonderful homes.

Grace, Stormy, and Sky Dancer were all set. But, what about Neebs? What would happen with him?

Chapter 16

LETTING GO

As each day passed, Abby felt more anxious about giving up the kittens. Ryan had grown attached to Neebs, too. Neebs followed him everywhere and even slept on Ryan's bed.

"Mom," Abby said as she sat on the living room floor watching the kittens playing with their toys, "I'm worried the kittens will be scared and miss us when they go to their new homes tomorrow."

She'd tossed and turned constantly the last couple of nights. She tried to picture the kittens happy in their new homes, but every time, her thoughts went back to the same worries.

Mom's knitting needles clicked together as she worked on an afghan. "I'm sure at first being in a new place will be a little scary for them," Mom said, "but they'll get so much attention and love, I'm sure they'll settle in quickly."

As if the kittens knew Abby was talking about them, they climbed down from the cat tree and grabbed toys. Sky Dancer picked up a small, green puffball and trotted around the room with it. Grace ran alongside her batting at it, but Sky Dancer managed to keep it securely in her mouth.

"What if the families don't have toys for them?" Abby asked. "The kittens love what we have."

Mom looked up, but her hands still worked the needles.

"When I visited, both families showed me where the kittens will sleep and the toys they have for them. They'll have cozy beds, a cat tree, and plenty of toys. I know it's hard, Abby, but you'll see. They'll be fine."

Abby swished a fluffy blue ball at the end of a wand along the carpet, hoping to get the kittens' attention. Grace ran through the cat tunnel to pounce while Neebs raced from his hiding spot next to the chair and jumped on the wand.

"Ahh!" she shrieked, pulling her hand back. Neebs rolled onto the floor with one paw on the toy. Stormy jumped on top of him and bit his neck.

"Hey! Be gentle!" Abby scolded, pulling Stormy off him. When he rolled over, she tickled his belly. "They're going to miss each other," Abby said. "They're used to lots of playmates."

Mom rested her knitting on her lap and looked up at Abby. "I have an idea," she said. "Why don't you make a special box to go with the kittens? We have a lot of toys, and each kitten seems to have favorites. You could send that box with them when they go to their new homes."

Abby jumped up from the floor. "That's a great idea! Maybe if they have familiar things, they won't be as scared. I'll put them together right now."

Abby went to the closet in the den where the empty boxes were stored. She picked out three and tossed them into the middle of the room. There was one for Grace, one for Neebs, and one for Stormy and Sky Dancer since they were going together.

When she closed the door and turned around, she discovered the kittens had followed her in and were climbing into the boxes. She laughed and shook her head.

"I'm going to miss you silly kitties."

Her throat tightened and she couldn't laugh anymore. Instead, she thought she might cry. Giving the kittens away was going to be the hardest thing she'd ever had to do.

She sat on the floor while the kittens climbed in and out of the boxes. Stormy launched over Abby's knee, then pounced on top of Sky Dancer in one box. They rolled and wrestled inside, looking like a big ball of fur. Grace jumped in and out of another like she was being chased.

Neebs jumped into the farthest box and laid down. He peeked his head up over the edge so only his pointy ears and his yellow eyes showed. He wanted to play hide-and-seek. Abby ducked a bit, then sat up quickly to play.

"Peek-a-boo, Neebs!"

The kitten quickly dropped his head below the edge. His ears still twitched within view.

"Where's Neebs?" Abby said in a sing-songy voice.

Neebs popped his head up again.

"Boo!" she said, and he dropped his face again. They played that game for a few minutes while the other kittens tumbled in the other boxes. The last time, Neebs waited longer to pop up. When he hadn't moved in a while, Abby raised up to look inside the box. The little black kitten was sound asleep with his chin on his paws.

"Meow!" Noelle came into the room and rubbed against Abby's arm.

"Hello, pretty girl," Abby said, stroking Noelle's back. "Did you come to check on your babies?"

Noelle scratched her cheek against the flap of each box. The girl kittens jumped out and climbed onto Abby's lap, but there wasn't enough room for all of them. She giggled as they flopped on the floor next to her, then scrambled to their feet and zoomed out of the room.

"Okay, little guy," she said to Neebs, "I'll make that box yours, but for right now, you need to get out of it."

She lifted Neebs out and gave him a snuggle before setting him on the floor. Then, she stacked the boxes together and carried them downstairs to the kitchen table. Using a dark marker, she wrote the kittens' names on the boxes. Next, she tore a piece of paper from a notebook and made a list of what she planned to include in each box.

She tapped the end of the pen against the paper, staring at her list. What could she send with the kittens that would smell familiar and maybe make them less scared in a new place? They loved to curl up next to her mom's slippers, but she couldn't give them those.

Then, she had an idea. She hurried into the living room.

She was surprised when she got there to see the kittens already curled up and sleeping. Grace and Stormy shared the top platform of the cat tree, while Noelle and Tanner slept on separate ones below. Sky Dancer was curled up in one of the cat beds on the floor with Chara.

She glanced around but didn't see Neebs. Her mom was still knitting on one end of the couch, and Ryan was stretched out under a blanket at the other end as he watched TV.

"Hmm," Abby said, wandering around the room and looking under furniture and into corners, "I wonder where Neebs is? It's weird that he didn't come in here with the other cats."

Mom smiled but didn't look up. "Oh, he did come in with them," she said.

"Really? Where is he?" Abby asked, confused. Was he behind the couch? He wasn't in sight, that was for sure.

Ryan giggled, and Abby whirled around in time to see him pull the blanket over his head.

"Ryan," she said, walking toward him, "do you know where Neebs is?"

"Nope!" he said, now laughing.

Abby grabbed the end of the blanket over Ryan's head and snapped it down toward his feet. Neebs' head popped up in surprise. He was curled against Ryan's side.

"He's my buddy," Ryan said. "I think he loves me."

Abby swallowed against the lump that popped into her throat. Ryan would be heartbroken when their mom finally found a new home for Neebs.

"It looks like he does love you," Abby said, fighting stinging in her eyes. But she couldn't think about that. She couldn't change that the kittens were leaving.

Tomorrow.

She had to focus on what she could do for them.

"Mom," she said, sitting on the arm of the chair, "I'm making a list of things to send with the kittens. I was thinking if we sent something that smells like Noelle and the other kittens, then maybe they wouldn't be so scared or lonely the first few nights in their new homes."

Mom looked up from her knitting. "That's a smart idea," she said. "Do you have something in mind?"

"I thought I could cut up the brown blanket they've slept on with Noelle since they were born. I'd send a piece with each of them. Would that be okay?"

Mom smiled and nodded. "Yes. That makes a lot of sense. You could add it to their boxes just before they leave. Maybe it could even go in their carriers."

"That's a good idea, too, Mom. Thanks!"

Abby returned to the kitchen to add to her list.

piece of brown blanket

She knew she might think of other things, but at least she had included the most important.

Her eyes welled up with tears again. How was she ever going to get through tomorrow?

Chapter 17

NEW HOMES

Abby rolled over in bed and opened her eyes. A thin line of light seeped past the side of the curtain and made a stripe on her wall.

How did this day get here so fast? It seemed like the kittens were just born. She moved her legs but bumped into a small body. Noelle. The cat had adopted Abby as her person, so she followed Abby everywhere. She had even started sleeping with Abby as if she was trying to get her kittens used to being without her.

Abby groaned and tried to ignore the fluttery feeling in her stomach. It had been there for the last two days. All she had to do was think about the kittens leaving, and it was like a whole bunch of butterflies had been released in her stomach.

She tried to take her mind off the feeling and what was happening today, but the butterfly thought wouldn't go away. What had Miss Loftus told her second grade class that a whole bunch of butterflies was called? She thought for a minute, then the word popped into her head.

"A kaleidoscope," she said out loud, even though Noelle was the only one who could hear her. She said the word again in her head as she pictured colorful butterflies. It sounded so pretty - except when it was happening in her stomach.

Her bedroom door opened a little, and her dad poked his head in.

"Hey, sleepyhead," he said, "the kittens' families will be here this morning. You want to get up and have breakfast before they arrive?"

Abby groaned again. "Yes. I'll be right down."

Food was the last thing she wanted to think about right now. She rolled to the edge of the bed, being careful to not disturb Noelle.

Today was no different. As soon as Abby was dressed and left her room, Noelle jumped down and trotted behind her down the stairs.

The kittens were already playing tag in and around the cat tunnel in the living room. Ryan was lying on his stomach with his face up close to one opening of the tunnel, encouraging them to run through toward him.

"Did you already have breakfast?" Abby asked him.

He pulled his head away from the end for a second. "Yeah!" Then, he went right back to playing.

Even though she'd rather play with the kittens, Abby moved on to the kitchen.

"Good morning," Mom said as she set a plate of French toast on the table. "It's a big day."

Mom sounded happy. How could she feel that way when the kittens were leaving forever?

"Mm-hmm," Abby responded, knowing words would get stuck in her throat if she tried to talk. She slid onto the chair and picked up the fork.

"Don't forget you want to cut pieces of the brown blanket to send with the kittens," Mom reminded her as she poured a glass of milk for Abby.

"I'll do that after breakfast," Abby said. The kaleidoscope of butterflies swirled in her stomach again. She took a couple of bites of French toast, but it was hard to swallow. She glanced at the clock.

She only had forty-five minutes left with the kittens she now loved.

With the French toast only half eaten, she set down the fork and took two swallows of her milk. It was all she could manage.

"Mom, I'm so sorry," she said, "but I'm not hungry."

Mom came over and sat in the chair next to Abby and put her hand on Abby's arm.

"If you're sad about the kittens leaving, Abby, I know it's hard, but wait until you see how loved they're going to be. I think it will help ease your worries. And, in a couple of weeks, after they've settled in, we'll visit them."

"I'm glad we can do that," Abby said. She picked up her plate and glass to carry to the sink. "I'm going to go get their blankets ready now."

She wanted to hurry from the kitchen before she burst into tears.

The O'Brien family arrived first. Mom invited them into the living room where the kittens were all worn out and had fallen asleep. Mom introduced Abby and Ryan to the parents and the two boys, Graham and Jamie.

Graham, the older one, looked like he might be eleven or twelve. He carried a big cat carrier that would hold two small kittens.

"You can set that right over here," Mom said, pointing to an area next to the couch. The boy set it down, then sat next to his parents and brother on the couch. Abby guessed his brother, Jamie, was about eight. Right in between her age and Ryan's.

While Mrs. O'Brien discussed vet appointments and other details about caring for the new family members, the boys stared at the kittens. Abby could tell they wanted to hold them.

"I see Stormy and Sky Dancer," Jamie said, pointing to the cat tree. The way he smiled and bounced a little on the couch, Abby knew he was excited. She would be, too, if she were getting new kittens.

As soon as she had that thought, the butterflies in her stomach settled a little. She remembered her mother saying that the O'Brien family had some sad things happen and that maybe having the kittens to love would help them feel better. It was obvious from the way Graham and Jamie sat on the edge of the couch smiling that the kittens were already making them happier. That made her feel better.

"Mom, is it okay if I bring the kittens over to Graham and Jamie?" she asked.

"Why don't you and Ryan each get one of them?" Dad suggested.

"Yeah," Ryan said, jumping up from the floor.

The kittens squeaked and stretched as soon as Ryan and Abby touched them. They gently lifted and cuddled them, then took them to the boys.

"I like the names you picked out for them," Abby said, setting Stormy on Graham's lap.

Ryan handed Sky Dancer to Jamie then stepped back. "She likes to play in the tunnel," he said. "Do you have a tunnel for them?"

Jamie snuggled Sky Dancer under his chin. "Yes, we do, and we have a cat tree that's even bigger than the one you have."

"Wow!" Ryan said. "They're going to love climbing all over that."

"And, we bought new toys for them, too," Graham said, stroking Stormy's head between her ears. The kitten responded by rolling her head against his fingers.

"We love Stormy and Sky Dancer already," Mrs. O'Brien said, as she reached over to pet both. "You don't have to worry. They're going to get so much attention and love."

Abby took a deep breath and felt her muscles relax. Even though she was sad to see the kittens leave, she could see this family already adored them.

"Did you see Neebs?" Ryan asked the boys. "He's the black kitten. He likes me best." He found Neebs sleeping at the base of the cat tree and scooped him up.

"He follows Ryan everywhere," Abby said as Ryan crossed the room.

Neebs squirmed in Ryan's arms until he nestled on Ryan's shoulder like a baby.

Ryan laughed. "He thinks he's a people baby. Sometimes I pretend to burp him." He lightly patted Neebs' back.

The doorbell rang, and Mollie started barking. Neebs scrambled out of Ryan's arms and scurried toward the kitchen. Stormy and Sky Dancer tried to run, too, but Graham and Jameson cuddled them closer.

"Mollie, stop barking!" Dad scolded as he went to greet the other family. Mollie raced past him down the front hall.

"Hello. Let's take you to meet your new family member," Abby heard her father say. Then, a few moments later, the couple followed Dad into the living room, with Mollie on their heels.

"This is Steve and Debbie Welnicki," Dad said, introducing them to the O'Briens. "They're adopting Grace, the little gray kitten."

"Aww," Debbie said when she saw Stormy and Sky Dancer with the boys, "they already look comfortable with you two."

"Abby," Mom said, "can you get Grace for Mr. and Mrs. Welnicki, please?"

Grace was snuggled next to Noelle and Neebs in the cat bed. A little stab of sadness washed over Abby again as she picked up the kitten. Even though giving these kittens new homes was the right thing to do, it didn't make it easier.

"Here you go," she said, as Mr. Welnicki took Grace and cuddled her against his chest. Grace mewed a couple of times and pushed back to stare up at him, but then she snuggled into his hands.

"You're going to be a very spoiled little kitty," Mrs. Welnicki said, petting Grace. "We bought you a new bed and all the toys you like here. You'll feel right at home."

A little more relief went through Abby. She was starting to feel like these people would love the kittens like her family did.

"Abby," Mom said, "why don't you get the special boxes you have for the families and kittens."

"Okay." She went to the hall to retrieve two of the three boxes. The one for Neebs would stay for now.

She set one box in front of the O'Briens and one in front of the Welnickis.

"I wanted to make sure the kittens wouldn't be too scared being away from us, so I put together these boxes with the food and toys that they like." She pulled out the piece of brown blanket from Stormy and Sky Dancer's box because it was bigger since there were two of them to share it.

"This is a piece of the blanket they've slept on with Noelle since they were born. We thought if they had this and it smelled familiar, maybe they would be more comfortable. I made it a good size to go in their carriers, too, for their trip today."

She handed Graham the piece of blanket, and he spread it in the carrier.

"Thank you," Mrs. O'Brien said. "This is a wonderful idea."

Mrs. Welnicki took the piece from Grace's box.

"Our carrier is in the hall," she said. "This is so thoughtful. We're worried about Grace being lonely at first, too. We'll give her lots of attention, but maybe this will make her feel more at home sooner. Thank you."

"You're all welcome," Abby said. Her worry melted into pride. She had done all she could to make sure the kittens still felt loved.

"Well," Mr. O'Brien said, slapping his palms against his legs. "I guess it's time to take these new family members home to meet our other cat and dog."

Abby watched as they put Stormy and Sky Dancer into the carrier. The kittens cowered into the back corner, as tight against each other as they could be.

The lump in her throat returned as the Welnickis did the same with Grace. Her heart pounded. It was hard to watch the two families walk down the hall to the front door with the kittens. Part of her wanted to run after them and take the kittens out of the carriers, but she held her hands together and stood back by the big window, instead.

As hard as it was to believe, in her heart she knew the kittens would be loved and taken care of. But it didn't make it any easier to see them leave.

Abby watched from the window, fighting tears. Noelle, Chara, Tanner, and Mollie surrounded her as if they knew she needed their support. She put her hand on her chest, wondering if the pain she felt in her heart was real or imagined. It didn't matter. If she felt this awful now, how would she feel when Neebs left?

Chapter 18

ESCAPEE

Abby didn't turn around from the window when she heard Ryan come back into the room and lie down on the couch. She didn't want him to see her eyes filled with tears. Watching three of the kittens leave with their new families was hard.

A moment later, the TV came on, and the voices of the scientists on one of Ryan's favorite shows filled the room.

"Wanna watch TV with me?" he asked. "Mom said if we watch Super Scientists, it will help us think about something else other than the kittens leaving."

Abby shook her head. Ryan's voice sounded sad, too. How could she watch TV when she hurt inside?

She picked up Noelle from the window ledge and hugged her.

"I'm sorry we couldn't keep your babies, Noelle," she whispered against the cat's head. "I know they'll have happy lives, though. And, I still have you and Chara and Tanner and Mollie." She sniffled. "And Neebs for a little while longer."

How long before he would go to a new home? She wondered if he was looking for his sisters right now.

She wiped her eyes with her sleeve, then turned around, still holding Noelle. She'd find Neebs and give the only kitten left plenty of attention.

She glanced around the room at all the usual places the kittens slept. He wasn't on the cat tree. He wasn't in the cat bed. She set Noelle down so she could get on her knees to look behind the couch, a favorite spot for the kittens when they were scared. He wasn't there, either.

"Ryan," she said, "have you seen Neebs?"

He sat up and glanced around the living room. "I saw him eating when the other kittens were leaving," he said, "but I haven't seen him since then."

"I haven't seen him, either," she said, suddenly feeling uneasy. "I'll check the pantry."

Mom and Dad were coming in from the front porch when Abby went down the hall.

"Are you doing okay, Ab?" Dad asked, wrapping her in a hug. "I know this is a hard thing to do, but those kittens are going to have a terrific life."

"I'm okay. It makes me really sad, but I know in my heart that they'll be loved." She sniffled and wiped her eyes again. "I'll be okay." She stepped back and looked toward her mom. "Right now, I'm trying to find Neebs."

"He's probably hiding," Mom said. "There was a lot of activity and strangers in the house."

"He's not in the living room," Abby said. "I'm going to check all of the kittens' other favorite spots."

"We'll help," Dad said. "Let's split up. Where's Ryan?"

"He's watching Super Scientists," Abby said.

"The three of us looking is enough for now, anyway," Mom said. "We'll find Neebs. He couldn't have gone far."

Abby started up the stairs. "I'll check up here. Neebs!" she called. "Neebs, come out, kitty. Come on, Neebs."

She heard her parents doing the same downstairs. The three of them checked every room, then switched places with each other to double check where the others had already looked.

More than twenty minutes later, they had covered every inch of the house. Neebs was nowhere to be found.

"Where could he have gone?" Abby asked, worried, as she went back to the pantry one more time to see if he had gone to eat.

"Kittens and cats are famous for finding little nooks and crannies to curl up in," Mom said. "Give him time, and I'm sure he'll come out to eat."

Abby shrugged. "I hope you're right."

"I'll make us lunch," Dad said. "Maybe the smell of food cooking will bring him out. Abby, can you take Mollie out for a few minutes, please?"

Abby went down the hall to the front door. She took her coat and boots from the closet on the way by.

"Mollie!" she called. "You wanna go out?"

She heard Mollie running from the living room, then laughed as she skidded around the corner.

"I guess that's a yes," Abby said, opening the front door.

Mollie jumped from the steps into the snowbank across the sidewalk. Abby followed down the steps and walked along the sidewalk as Mollie raced back and forth in the snow.

After a few minutes, she called Mollie back in. She had just lifted her foot onto the first step when something caught her eye between the stair railing and bush.

She leaned down to look closer at the snow. Her heart jumped. Cat pawprints! A wave of panic zinged through her chest. No! These weren't pawprints from a full-sized cat. These pawprints were much smaller. She was positive these tracks were made by kitten-sized paws.

Abby's hands started to shake.

Neebs had escaped.

Chapter 19

PAWPRINTS ON THE HEART

"Mollie! In!" Abby ordered as she raced up the front steps. She opened the door and Mollie charged in ahead of her.

"Mom! Dad!" she yelled, racing in behind her. "Neebs escaped!" Her panic raised the pitch of her voice. The snow on her boots dropped onto the wooden floor and one foot slipped, almost causing her to fall. "He's outside somewhere."

Her parents and Ryan nearly collided as they hurried into the hallway.

"Neebs is outdoors?" Ryan asked, his eyes wide. He rushed to the door to look out the window. "He's too little to be outdoors in the snow."

"How do you know he's outside?" Mom asked.

Abby backed toward the door while she answered. "Because I saw kitten pawprints in the snow. They're too small to be Noelle's. I have to go out and look for him."

"Me, too," Ryan said. He scurried back to the closet to get his coat and boots.

"We'll be right out, too," Mom said.

"Be careful where you walk," Dad added. "You don't want to wipe away any pawprints."

"He must be so cold," Abby said as she ran out the door.

"Wait for me!" Ryan yelled. But he didn't even have his boots on. There was no time to wait.

She walked along the sidewalk while keeping an eye on the pawprints. They went through the snow between the back of the bushes and the porch. She was thankful the leaves were off the bushes so she could easily track the pawprints.

"Neebs! Come here, kitty," she called over and over. "Where are you?"

The front door slammed open, and Ryan burst out. "Did you find him?"

He jumped from the top step down onto the sidewalk then ran to Abby.

"Not, yet. I'm following his pawprints. Be careful where you walk," she cautioned.

The prints followed the whole line of the front porch, then suddenly ended at the sidewalk.

"Oh, no!" Abby said, turning halfway around. "Neebs came out onto the sidewalk here —" she pointed where the snow met the sidewalk — "but where did he go from here?"

She looked at the snow across the sidewalk from where the kitten had left the snow by the bushes. She groaned when she realized Mollie had run through that area when they'd first come out. Abby and Ryan split to look in different areas but saw no clear evidence that Neebs had gone to the other side of the sidewalk.

"Let's look at the end of the sidewalk by the driveway to see if we can find his tracks again," Abby suggested.

Ryan looked on one side and Abby looked on the other. Their parents come out the door behind them.

"Any luck?" Dad asked as they approached.

"We lost the tracks when he came out onto the sidewalk," Abby said, feeling frustrated. "I don't even know where to look now."

"I'll go around the house," Dad said.

"It doesn't look like he went up the maple tree in the front yard," Mom pointed out. "With no leaves, it's pretty easy to see."

"Is he going to freeze to death?" Ryan asked.

Abby spun toward her mother. "What if we never see him again?"

A horrified look crossed Ryan's face. "I don't want anything to happen to him. We have to find him."

Mom put her hand on Ryan's shoulder. "We'll keep looking, Ryan. We all want to find him."

Abby turned back to the snow along the driveway. "Hey! I think I found his tracks, again," she said a couple of minutes later. "He must be having a hard time walking in this snow, so he can't be far."

Abby took the lead following the pawprints. In a couple of places Mollie's tracks wiped them out, but then she found Neebs' prints again and continued tracking.

They went under the bird feeder by the shed. Had Neebs been after birds? It took a few more minutes to find the tracks again, but when Abby found them, she followed them straight to a pine tree.

She looked all around the base but saw no tracks away from the tree.

"The tracks stop here," she said, parting branches. "Neebs! Neebs, are you here?" she called.

Ryan dropped to his belly to crawl on the ground under the lowest branches.

"I see them! I see his pawprints under here," Ryan exclaimed. "Neebs! Little buddy, where are you?" he called.

"Mew!"

They all stopped and froze.

"Mew!"

The sound came from the tree. Abby moved more of the poking branches but couldn't get in close.

Suddenly Ryan yelled. "He's here! I found him!"

The pine needles scratched Abby's face as she tried to get in closer to Neebs.

"Mew! Mew!" the kitten cried again.

"I can't get in there," Abby said. "There are too many branches." She peeked through and saw a patch of his black fur.

"I can reach him," Ryan said, pulling himself up along the inside of the tree trunk.

Abby squatted so she could see Ryan and Neebs. The branches were thick and prickly, but she and her dad parted them, so Ryan had more room to work.

"Mew!" Neebs cried again.

"You're okay, Neebs," Ryan reassured the kitten.

He reached through the branches and plucked Neebs from the tree.

"Ow!" Ryan yelled. "His claws are digging into my hands."

"Hold him against your coat," Mom suggested.

Ryan tucked him inside his coat to warm him up.

"I need to get out of these branches," Ryan said, working his way through the branches that jabbed and poked him at every move. He used his arm to protect Neebs from getting scratched by the sharp pine needles.

"Mew!" Neebs complained under Ryan's coat.

Mom peeked in at the kitten, then guided Ryan away from the tree.

"Let's get this little troublemaker inside," she said. "This was one scare too many."

Once inside, Abby slipped out of her coat. "I can't believe he got out," she said. "I wonder how it happened."

"He must have sneaked out in all the commotion of the families leaving with the other three kittens," Mom said. "We were all so distracted, it was easy for him to go right by us."

Dad was the last one through the front door. Once it was closed, Ryan set Neebs down on the floor. The kitten scampered down the hall and into the living room. They followed, happy to see the other three cats and Mollie napping as if there hadn't just been a crisis.

Abby sat cross-legged on the floor next to Noelle. "When we find a family for Neebs, we'll have to warn them that he likes to sneak out," she said. "I was so scared that it distracted me from thinking about the other kittens leaving."

Mom sat in one chair and Dad sat in another. Ryan sat on the floor, trying to coax Neebs to come to him, but the kitten wanted to lie next to Noelle.

"It looks like Neebs is happy to be back inside where he's warm and safe," Dad said. "Hopefully he realizes that it's much better and safer for him in the house."

Abby stretched forward to pet Noelle and Neebs.

"I hope his next family loves him as much as we do," she said.

Mom nodded. "I think we all got attached to all of the kittens. I was just as sad as you were about them leaving."

"I know," Abby said. She petted Noelle, who made a happy chirping noise then stretched out next to Abby's leg. "I'm lucky that you said I could keep Noelle. I think she's kind of attached to me. She follows me everywhere."

Dad chuckled. "We've noticed that. It's like you two were meant to be together."

Abby smiled. "We are. I love Chara and Tanner, too, but they belong to our whole family. Noelle adopted me."

Mom nodded. "It seems sometimes animals pick their person."

Dad cleared his throat. Abby looked up in time to see Mom and Dad exchange a smile.

Dad leaned forward in the chair with his arms resting on his legs.

"Abby, Mom and I have been thinking about how responsible you've been with Noelle and the kittens. We're very proud of you."

Abby's cheeks warmed. She knew she was blushing.

"Thank you." She didn't know what else to say. She hadn't expected that compliment.

"So," Mom said, "we've made a decision. You were very brave when the other kittens left today. We know how hard it's been for you as you prepared for them to leave."

"It's been really hard. Sometimes I felt like my heart was being pulled out of my chest." She could feel the sting of salty tears behind her eyes again.

"Well, even though we hadn't planned this, we've decided we're not going to look for a family for Neebs," Mom said.

Abby wiped her eyes with the back of her hand. "What do you mean? What are we going to do with him?"

"He'll stay right here," Dad explained. "He can be yours, too."

Abby gasped and covered her mouth with one hand. "Forever?"

Mom and Dad smiled as they nodded.

Everything inside Abby brightened. She didn't have to stand in the window and watch another kitten leave. Her face heated up even more, but this time because of her big smile.

She turned to Ryan, feeling happier than she had in a long time. But the look on his face caused her smile to droop. She thought he'd be happy that Neebs was staying. He loved Neebs. Whenever she looked for Neebs lately, she always found him curled up with Ryan or playing with him.

Then a lightbulb went off in her head.

Abby pushed her tongue against the inside of her mouth as she quickly decided. She looked back at her parents.

"I don't think I can keep Neebs," she said.

Mom and Dad looked back and forth at each other, clearly confused.

"But we thought you'd be thrilled to keep him," Mom said.

Abby picked up the sleepy Neebs and held him against her shoulder. He squeaked and moaned, but never opened his eyes.

"I *am* thrilled," Abby said. "Neebs is an awesome kitten, and I'd love to be his person, but Noelle has already picked me, so I can't keep him for myself."

"What do you mean?" Dad asked, looking shocked.

"We all know Mollie's person is you, Dad," Abby explained. "If we look for her, we usually find her with you. Right?"

He nodded. "Yes, I suppose that's true."

"And Tanner and Chara are like a matched pair because they like to sit with you, Mom."

"I never thought about it, but I guess you're right," Mom said.

"Well, they picked you, just like Noelle picked me." Abby looked at Ryan. "But, when we're looking for Neebs, where do we usually find him?"

Ryan perked up and sat straighter, using his thumb to point to his chest. "With me!"

"Yes," Abby said, holding Neebs out toward Ryan. "Neebs has picked *you* to be his person, not me."

A grin filled Ryan's face. "You're giving me your kitten?" he asked.

Abby shook her head. "No, he's not mine. He never was. He's always been yours. I was just taking care of him for you."

Ryan smiled as he gently rocked Neebs. "He picked *me* to be his person?"

"That's right. Just like Noelle's pawprints in the snow led me to her, Neebs' pawprints in the snow led you to him. I think that's a sign," Abby said.

Ryan cuddled Neebs against his chest.

Abby smiled. For a day that had started out with such a heavy feeling on her heart, it had all turned around. With Stormy, Sky Dancer and Grace in new, loving homes, and Noelle and Neebs now part of the family, everything felt right.

Abby looked around at the content animals and her loving family and realized something important. The pawprints in the snow would melt someday, but the pawprints the cats and kittens left on their hearts would last a lifetime.

About the Author

Laurie Gifford Adams grew up on a dairy farm in the Finger Lakes of western New York. She was born with a love for all animals, and over the years has given a home to dogs, cats, horses, rabbits, gerbils, a guinea pig, a chicken, and a parakeet. Noelle isn't the first stray cat Laurie has adopted, and probably won't be the last. Many of her family's pets over the years have been rescues they adopted from shelters, and they've never regretted the decision.

Visit Laurie's website to learn more about her and her other books: www.lauriegiffordadams.com

About the Illustrator

Nissa Burch is a self-taught artist from a small town outside of Rochester, NY. She has always admired the way the world looks and creating a bigger perspective of what not many pay attention to. She's been creating for about 10 years with more to come. Pawprints in the Snow is the first book Nissa has illustrated.

To learn more about her, visit her website:
https://nissaburch.wixsite.com/website

Laurie Gifford Adams

SNAPSHOTS

Made in United States
Orlando, FL
29 November 2021